cITY·of·THe
DEAD

CITY·OF·THE
DEAD

SHARON·STEWART

Red Deer PRESS

The Publishers
Red Deer Press
MacKimmie Library Tower
University Drive N.W.
Calgary Alberta Canada T2N 1N4

Credits
Edited for the Press by Peter Carver
Cover and text design by Duncan Campbell
Cover photograph courtesy of Mark Tomalty/Masterfile
Printed and bound in Canada by Friesens for Red Deer Press

Acknowledgments
Financial support provided by the Canada Council,
the Department of Canadian Heritage, the Alberta Foundation for the Arts,
a beneficiary of the Lottery Fund of the Government of Alberta,
and the University of Calgary.

National Library of Canada Cataloguing in Publication Data

Stewart, Sharon (Sharon Roberta), 1944–
City of the dead
ISBN 0-88995-229-9
I. Title.
PS8587.T4895C57 2001   C813'.54   C2001-910209-7
PR9199.3.S79452C57 2001

5   4   3   2   1

To Roderick, for all the reasons.

contents

1. Dog Days—1

2. Trojan Horse—23

3. Call Me—42

4. The Village—59

5. Cade—80

6. Dingbat—113

7. Lucky Seven—137

8. Hooked—157

9. Flying Toasters—185

10. City of the Dead—202

DOG • DAYS

"Now, that's what I call tacky. *Really* tacky!"

Mom was standing by the kitchen door with a bunch of flyers in her hand. Normally, she takes a direct approach with junk mail and dumps it straight into the recycling box. But something about one of the pieces had caught her eye.

"Will, take a look at this," she said, giving Dad a nudge on the shoulder to rouse him from his deep-sea dive into the morning paper.

"C'mon, Mom," I moaned for about the sixth time. I couldn't seem to get through to her that, yes, I had put my school jeans in the wash on Saturday, and, no, I hadn't seen them since. Which was why I was standing in the kitchen in my T-shirt and undershorts at twenty-five minutes to nine on the first day of school.

"Hmmm?" She was still leaning over Dad's shoulder pointing out something in the flyer.

"Jeans, Mom. Please. J-E-A-N-S. Where are they?"

"In the dryer, Mark. Where do you think?" Then, "Is it for real?" she said to my dad.

He shrugged. "Must say I haven't seen this kind of thing before. But, hey, everything else is turning up in the junk mail these days. Banks, lawyers. Medical clinics even. So why not?"

I didn't hear the rest of what was said because I'd hotfooted it downstairs to the dryer. Sure enough, there were the jeans. About two sizes smaller. I wish I could get through to Mom not to dry them on high. I'd be walking stiff-legged all day.

A dog was trotting by as I wheeled my bike out of the garage.

"Hi, fella," I said and snapped my fingers at him just to be polite. He was a strange-looking beast. Jet black with a pointy nose and big bat ears that stood straight up. Long slender legs tapering to neat paws. He wore a narrow red collar with a heavy gold tag on it. Probably some kind of Doberman, I figured, though I didn't remember Dobermans having brushy tails like this dog's.

The dog was polite, too. He gave me a quick glance, running out his long red tongue and showing off a really healthy-looking set of white teeth. But he wasn't the least bit interested in me. He kept right on going—a dog with purpose, minding his own business.

I shot down the hill on my bike and didn't give the dog a further thought.

Until he turned up on the school grounds. A bunch of us guys were hanging around, trying to postpone the evil moment when we had to give up the last of our summer freedom and head into the school.

"Uh-oh," said Jeremy Wong, glancing back at the street.

It took only a second for the rest of us to get the drift. Butcher Baker and a couple of his goons were slouching in our direction. The scowls on their faces looked particularly hideous in the crystal-clear September sunlight. I'm sure I don't have to tell you much to clue you in to the kind of guy Butcher was, and how he came by his nickname. Every school on the planet probably has one of his type. Way back in Grade One he'd started pushing kindergarten kids into mud puddles and stealing their lunch money. He'd long since moved on to nastier things.

"I told you he wouldn't forget about what you did last spring, Mark-o," said Jeremy, nudging me in the ribs. Jeremy's my best friend, and no one enjoys the scrapes I get myself into more than he does.

"Yeah," I breathed, breaking out in a light sweat. I might as well tell you right up front that I have this terrible weakness: I like to play practical jokes on people. And the more awful the people, the harder it is for me to resist the temptation. Butcher Baker was prime, Grade A, practical joke material. Unfortunately, he didn't get much of a laugh out of the contact cement I'd put into his gym shorts. He'd threatened to kill me, in fact. Luckily, summer had intervened, and I'd hoped he'd mellow out over the holidays. He lived on the other side of town, and I'd made sure our paths didn't cross.

So he and his buddies were probably on their way over to rearrange my features. Then the dog showed up. He loped across the school grounds and fetched up beside Butcher just as he loomed over me. The dog sat down at his feet and looked up at him, laughing.

Then Butcher had me by the collar. "Any last words, clown?" he growled, shaking me the way a cat does a mouse.

"Nice dog you have there," I squeaked.

"Huh?"

I pointed.

Butcher's brows drew together like hairy black clouds, and he aimed a kick at the animal. "Not mine, stupid," he said, giving me another shake.

The dog didn't seem to agree. He danced agilely away from the kick, then sat down again, still grinning.

Just then the bell rang. Butcher gave me a final shake. "Don't get your hopes up. I'll deal with you later," he snarled, dropping me.

We all walked toward the school. The dog got up and followed Butcher, who ignored him.

"Nice doggy," said Ms. Garnett, the teacher who had drawn door duty. "Nice doggy. But you can't come in. Go home."

She reached down to pat him. Then, as the dog looked up at her, she jerked her hand back. I don't know why, really. He didn't growl or anything. He just gave her a considering kind of look. Then his eyes zapped back to Butcher, who was disappearing down the hall.

Ms. Garnett closed the door in the dog's face, and that was that.

We got right into all that wonderful first-day stuff you have to go through every school year. I wasn't too thrilled to find out that Butcher and I were in the same homeroom. That was definitely not going to make life any easier.

Jeremy, the rat, thought it was funny. "Dum-dum-da-DUM, dum-da-DUM-da-DUM-da-DUM," he hummed under his breath. The tune of a famous funeral march.

Yeah, right. I mean, what are friends for?

I landed a seat near the door, my first piece of good luck that day. It meant I'd at least be able to make a fast-breaking getaway at the end of class. It was something.

We were all looking over our new texts, getting a feel for the horrors to come, when Lolita Bailey got up and left the room. I mean, she'd hardly got there and already she had to go. Well, that's Lolita. Anyway, she didn't close the door behind her. And pretty soon I heard this sound, sort of like "clickety-tickety-pick." A toenail-on-linoleum kind of sound, coming closer. Then a pointy black nose and a pair of space-launch ears appeared in the doorway. The dog had arrived.

Catching sight of him, our homeroom teacher, Bernie Berndorf, paused in midsentence. The dog gave him the once-over, then tick-tacked his way over to Butcher's desk. There he sat down and ran out his tongue, laughing.

"Well. Quite an amazing-looking beast," Old Man Berndorf said. "But you know better than to bring him to school, Sylvester. Like Mary's little lamb, you know. It's against the rule."

We all snickered.

Sylvester was Butcher's real name, though he didn't much like to be called by it. His mother must have watched too many old Sylvester Stallone movies before he was born.

Butcher's jaws clamped shut. "It's not my dog. Nothin' to do with me," he grated.

"Sir," prodded Old Man Berndorf.

"Sir."

"Well, he seems to think he's yours. Please take him outside. Now."

Butcher got up, scowling, and lumbered over to the door. The

5

dog got up and followed close behind him, and the two of them disappeared into the hall.

The dog must have got the message that enough was enough, because he didn't show up inside the school again. But he was waiting right outside for Butcher when school let out. I know because I passed him at full speed.

"Hi, pooch," I called as I grabbed my bike.

He jumped to his feet when he caught sight of Butcher pounding down the stairs after me. He didn't bark or anything, but his brushy tail began to wag slowly back and forth. No accounting for taste, a classy-looking dog like that falling for Butcher Baker. But I had other things to worry about just then. Like putting on some serious speed so I could live another day.

When I got home, I went to the fridge and chugalugged a liter of orange juice to cool off. The flyer Mom and Dad had been talking about was lying on the counter. I turned it over idly, wondering what had got Mom's dander up.

The flyer was bordered in black, and there was the image of a pointed, triangular thing in the middle. Above it were the words Obelisk Services. Underneath, it read, *The Rite Choice. Multicultural Funeral Functions Available.* There was some fine print at the bottom that I didn't bother to read. I mean, the rest was gross enough. Imagine advertising a funeral service through the mail! It was enough to give you the creeps. For once, my mom and I were on the same wavelength.

I shivered and chucked the flyer in the trash.

Well, the next day, Butcher arrived back at school with the dog. This time the beast seemed content to stay outside. Maybe he'd figured out that the object of his affection was locked up safely and couldn't get away. Anyhow, when I happened to look out the hall window between classes, there he was, lying crouched on his belly with his front paws stretched straight out. He looked like some kind of weird stone garden ornament.

Butcher's pals were razzing him.

"Your dog's still there, man," I overheard one of them say.

Butcher didn't seem too happy about it. "I keep telling ya, it's not my dog."

"Yeah, man, but it thinks it is," someone else said.

"Aw, shut up about it," said Butcher, rolling his shoulders the way he does when he's looking around for somebody to beat on.

I faded into the background, making sure I stayed inconspicuous. That dog was okay by me. It seemed to have taken his mind off the contact cement. I was hoping that if Butcher forgot about it long enough, he'd find himself another victim.

The next day, Butcher didn't show up at school. The office sent up a note to Old Man Bernsdorf that made his eyebrows shoot right up to his hairline. What there was left of it.

We serfs all exchanged glances. What was going on?

He cleared his throat and said, "Settle down, all of you. We'll be hearing a special announcement from the office any minute."

Right on cue, the P.A. system warbled, then the principal's voice said, "Students, I'm sincerely sorry to have to make this announcement. It is with deep regret that I report the death of one of your schoolmates—Sylvester Baker. He died yesterday afternoon in a most unfortunate accident. Let's spend a moment of silence in honor of Sylvester, remembering him as our friend and classmate."

Unfortunately, the P.A. system picked that moment to emit a piercing squeal, which spoiled the effect. Not that most of us had any happy memories of Butcher to reflect on anyway. I mean, even the teachers must have had feelings of relief. How could they help it? They're human, too. Sort of.

I sneaked my lucky rabbit's foot out of my pocket and kissed it. "Way to go," I muttered to it. Butcher's life might be over, but I felt as if mine was just beginning.

There was a lot of buzz afterward, of course. Everybody wondering what happened and all. At noon, a bunch of us tore over to the paper box at the corner and bought all the newspapers we could find. Even some of the teachers did.

"Here it is!" someone yelped.

Butcher had made page one in both papers. "Local teen killed in freak accident," read one headline. "Tragic death of boy blamed on faulty equipment," read the other.

To give you the short version, some movers had dropped a grand piano on Butcher. From four floors up. Believe me, you don't want to know any more details than that.

Nobody did.

"Yuck," someone said.

"Gross," said somebody else.

Nobody felt like eating lunch.

At three o'clock the P.A. came on again. "Sylvester Baker's parents have informed me that funeral services will be held at two-thirty tomorrow afternoon at the Obelisk Services chapel in Paramount Road," the principal announced. "In view of how close we all felt to Sylvester, anyone wishing to attend will be excused from class for the afternoon."

A half-holiday! For the first time, I truly had warm feelings about Butcher.

"I just hope it's a closed casket," I whispered to Jeremy.

He turned green and looked away.

Anyway, of course everybody went. Who wouldn't, to get off school? The chapel was pretty crowded. It was an impressive-looking place with lots of stone pillars and a high ceiling. Right in the middle of the entrance hall was the pointy object I'd seen on the flyer. In real life it was massive, at least ten feet tall and made out of polished black granite.

"Hey, an obelisk," said Pete Kuriyan. He's the class brain and always knows the right words for things. "Cool."

I shrugged. "I guess. If you go for that kind of thing." Personally, I thought it looked creepy. Like something you'd put on Dracula's grave to keep the old vamp from getting out to terrorize the peasants. Whatever was buried under a hunk of rock like that would stay planted.

There was this slick-looking guy in charge of everything. Tall, dark and handsome in a wiry kind of way. He had a real dark tan—he must have spent a lot of time in Florida. I could see some of the girls checking him out and whispering to each other. If he hadn't been a funeral director, they'd have been drooling all over him.

I overheard the guy introducing himself to the principal. "My name is Cyrus," he said, shaking hands. "I'm the proprietor of Obelisk Services. I'm sure Sylvester's parents will appreciate seeing so many of his classmates here today. It was most kind of you to let them out of school."

The principal nodded, gazing up at him. It looked to me as though Cyrus held her hand just a second longer than he really needed to. And she liked it. I keep forgetting she's a woman.

After the service, we milled around for a while, wondering what to do. Someone mentioned meeting back at the school to shoot a few hoops, but it didn't seem right after a funeral. Even if it was Butcher's funeral. So we drifted off home.

It was a couple of weeks before I saw the dog again. I had to go across town for something, and I happened to pass by Greenwillow Common. It sounds grand, but it's really just a big open field with a couple of tall willow trees. Anyway, right out in the middle of the field was this little kid, throwing a ball in the air. Then I saw the dog. He seemed to float up into the air and grab the ball at an impossible height before returning to the ground. Then he bounded back to the boy carrying the ball.

It was the same dog. Had to be—you couldn't miss those ears. The whole performance was like watching a movie in slow motion: the flight of the ball, the dog's leap, his easy lope back to the kid. And in the background the long green hair of the willows waving in the wind.

Something, who knows what, made me get off my bike and walk across the field toward them. This time the dog looked at me for a long moment, as though he remembered me and was giving me his full consideration. Then his eyes snapped back to the kid.

"Uh, hi. This your dog?" I asked.

"I'm not supposed to talk to strangers," the kid said, frowning.

"Well, I'm not strange, am I? Weird, maybe, but strange, no."

That got a trace of a grin out of him. I'm no expert on kids, but he was a nice-looking little guy with dark hair that could have used a trim and big brown eyes.

The dog pranced with his front paws, so the kid threw the ball again. The dog shot away after it.

"He's not my dog," the kid said. "He just started following me today. I can't take him home, though. We live in an apartment."

"I've seen him around before," I said. "I guess he's a stray."

"No," said the kid, shaking his head. "I checked the tag on his collar. His name and a phone number are on it. It's a funny name."

The dog bounded up and dropped the ball at the boy's feet.

"Here, boy. Let me see your tag," I said to him, bending down and reaching for it.

He gave me a look, and I pulled my hand back. Somehow I didn't feel like grabbing him by the collar, either. His expression just didn't invite meddling. But the kid apparently didn't feel that way. He took hold of the dog's gold tag and said, "His name is A-N-U-B-I-S. What does that spell?"

"I dunno," I replied. "Well, maybe you should phone the number and let the owner know he's running loose. So the pound won't pick him up."

"I guess so," said the kid. "Maybe I'll just throw the ball for him a few more times first."

"Why not?" I said. "Enjoy." I walked back to my bike leaving the two of them there.

A couple of days later, my mom surprised me by walking into my room after she got home from work and giving me a big hug.

I eased my way out of it. "Hey, cool it, Mom. Hold the mush." I peered at her and could see that her eyelids were a bit red and puffy. "Aw, you haven't been crying, have you?"

"A little. Oh, Markie, you'll think I'm crazy, but there was such a sad story in the paper. A little boy who drowned. His mother's only child. A terrible thing. And . . . and . . . I couldn't help thinking how I'd feel. . . ."

Her voice trembled a little. For a hotshot lawyer, my mom can be a real softie. I was sorry she was upset, but, jeez, I wish she wouldn't call me Markie.

After she left, I puzzled about it a bit. Another dead body? That was two within a month. Our little town was pretty deadly in a lot of ways, but not, like, literally. Then I shrugged. Okay, it was odd, but not all that odd—was it? Still, I somehow couldn't get the story out of my head. Even trigonometry couldn't cast its usual spell over me. So I padded down to my mother's office. "Mom, that story. Do you still have the paper?"

"Right there in my briefcase."

I dug out the paper and took it into the kitchen. I flipped through a couple of pages and there it was. "Child found drowned in apartment building pool," read the headline. And there was a photo. "Fernando Hernandez, age 7," according to the caption. A cute kid, with longish hair and big dark eyes. The same one I'd seen at the common. With Anubis.

I froze, staring down at the picture while my mind ran that slow-motion movie again—the boy, the leaping dog, the wind, the trees. And ran it again.

Aw, c'mon, I told myself. It's just a coincidence. It has to be. But somehow I couldn't get rid of the knot in my stomach. The coincidence was more than strange. It was downright spooky.

I couldn't stop thinking about it the rest of the day. That's another weakness of mine, you see. Like the practical jokes. I have to niggle away at things until I get them figured out.

I told Jeremy about it at school the next day. Now, there aren't too many people I'd tell about a thing like that. I mean, you could easily get a rep as a loony-tune. But I can trust old Jeremy.

He was totally cool about it all. "So what's happened, really?" he asked sensibly. "There's a stray dog . . ."

"Not a stray dog. He's got a collar tag with his name and phone number on it."

"Okay, okay. Not a stray, but allowed to run loose. He happens to follow Butcher around for a while. Another time you see him with that little kid. Both of them die later. So what?"

"Yeah, yeah. But there's something weird about that dog, Jeremy."

He rolled his eyes. "So he's got big ears. Big deal."

I felt a bit better after I talked to Jeremy. But I couldn't stop myself from checking out the funeral notices in the paper that evening. I soon wished I hadn't. "Hernandez, Fernando," one small notice read. "Only son of Maria Felita Lopez de Hernandez. Memorial service at Obelisk Services, 100 Paramount Road, 20 September at 5:00 p.m."

I was on the phone to Jeremy in two seconds flat. "Listen, something weird really is going on," I babbled.

Jeremy heard me out, then sighed. "Man, you're losing it," he said. "So the poor kid's mother got a flyer in the mail. Like, you know, junk mail. And if a person suddenly needs a funeral home—well, Obelisk is probably as good as any other business. It looked like a pretty classy place. So what's your problem?"

I hung up and mulled it over, shifting up through all my mental gears. What *was* my problem? So the dog had showed up with two people who both died later. But they didn't die of dog bites, did they? Probably the dog hung out with all sorts of people who went right on living, including its owner. Jeremy was right. I must be losing it.

I decided to try to forget the whole thing. I tried out for the football team that week and actually made it. That helped a lot. Being trampled on a daily basis by a herd of buffalo in cleats kind of takes your mind off other things.

My dad was so thrilled by my nonexistent prowess that it was almost touching. He kept retelling all his old quarterback stories from college and wanting to throw passes in the back yard. Luckily for me, he was helping out the folks across the street quite a lot. Our elderly neighbor, Mr. Henderson, had had a nasty fall and was bedridden. My dad's a freelance writer, so he's home most of the time. He'd volunteered to help Mrs. Henderson get her husband in and out of bed, and so on. He also used to go over and have a cup of tea with them in the late afternoon, which got him off my back.

So I was feeling sore but otherwise pretty good about life when I limped home late one October afternoon after football practice. Our house was dark, so I knew Dad must still be across the street. I glanced over at the Hendersons'. The porch light was on, and it shone down the path to the front gate. There was just enough light to see something crouching in the shadows inside the fence. Something with a pointy face and bat ears.

Anubis.

So he was still wandering around loose. I took a deep breath.

There's no way you're going to let yourself be spooked again, I told myself. So I decided to brazen it out. I crossed the street and leaned over the gate, giving a sharp whistle through my teeth.

"Hey, Anubis. How are you, boy? Chased any balls lately?"

The ears twitched and the pointy muzzle swiveled toward me in the dusk. Then the dog got up and came right over, putting his front paws up on the gate. This time he greeted me like an old buddy, running out his tongue and laughing up at me, his tail moving to and fro in elegant sweeps. The faint light reflected in his eyes, giving them a weird golden glow in his black face. I took a step backward—I couldn't help myself. Then the front door opened and the dog's attention shot back to it.

Dad was leaving. Anubis trotted up the path and climbed the steps to the porch.

"Well, hello there," said Dad, in a cosy talking-to-dogs tone of voice. "My, you're a fine-looking fellow. Who do you belong to?" Then, when the dog tried to push past him into the house, "No, you can't go in there. Go home, boy. There's a good dog."

Anubis faded back into the shadows of the yard, but I was pretty sure he didn't leave. It gave me an awful bad feeling about Mr. Henderson.

Dad put his arm around my shoulder as we walked back across the street. "Practice go okay, son?"

"Yeah, fine. Might even get a chance to get off the bench one of these games. Uh, Dad?"

"Hmmm?"

"Mr. Henderson. Is he, like, okay?"

"Not so good, actually. He seems to be developing a slight

case of pneumonia. Probably from being bedridden for so long. The doctor's got him on antibiotics for a few days. That should fix him up."

I had a sinking feeling that it wouldn't. And sure enough, the next day the ambulance arrived and carried Mr. Henderson off to the hospital, siren wailing. The day after that he died.

I felt sorry for him and for poor Mrs. Henderson, of course. But it was the thought of Anubis lurking around outside their house like some kind of ghoul that put a serious chill down my spine.

I probably don't have to tell you where the funeral services were held. My family went, of course, what with Dad being so close to the Hendersons and all. Cyrus was there, looking as sleek as ever, doing his PR number.

"My, what a good-looking man," my mom murmured to my dad. "He's as handsome as a god!"

Personally, I didn't see it. Dad looked as if he didn't get it either.

It was on the way out that I saw Anubis crossing the other end of the hall. I wasn't even surprised.

Cyrus, who was shaking hands with my parents, caught me staring at the dog.

"That's Anubis," he said, smiling.

"I've seen him around," I said.

"Me, too," Dad put in. "Outside the Hendersons' house in our street the other night."

Cyrus shook his head regretfully. "I just can't keep him from wandering. He always manages to find a way out."

"Really," I said.

Cyrus turned to my mom. "It's been a great pleasure to meet

you. By the way, here's my card."

Mom took it in a dazed sort of way. She looked as if she was drowning in those big dark eyes of his.

When we got home, she went over and carefully propped the card up on the mantel.

Dad snorted. "Hey, whose funeral are you planning anyway?" he wanted to know.

I kind of wondered, too. That card looked pretty ominous sitting there.

"Hmmm?" she asked, looking kind of dreamy.

Why some guys have that effect on women, I'll never know.

Anyway, the next day I told Jeremy about it all. "I *know* there's something going on," I fretted. "There has to be. This dog-and-death thing has happened too many times to be coincidence. And the services are always at Obelisk."

"Listen. You said the guy admits his dog wanders around a lot," Jeremy pointed out. "I still don't think there's anything weird about it. Cyrus advertises; people call him to arrange funerals. Not my idea of a dream job, but someone has to do it. I just don't get what's eating you."

"It's a feeling," I told him. "I can't explain it. Something about the dog. But one thing I do know. I'm going to find out what's going on."

"How?" demanded Jeremy.

"For starters, I'm going over there tonight to have a look."

Jeremy shook his head. "You're nuts, man. You'll probably get arrested for trespassing. What do you think you're going to find anyway?"

"I haven't a clue," I admitted. "But something's fishy about the whole setup."

"You know, Mark-o, I really think you should drop this thing," said Jeremy. "What are you trying to prove? That the dog's a homicidal maniac or something?"

His sweet reason just made me feel more twitchy. I shrugged. "Don't ask—it's just a crazy hunch. And you know me, man: I just can't leave anything alone until I get to the bottom of it. Anyway," I went on, "are you coming with me?"

Old Jeremy's hair practically stood on end. "Me? Sneak around a funeral home at night? There might be, like, dead bodies! You've got to be kidding. Include me out."

What a pal.

It wasn't hard to convince my parents that I had to be out that evening. I cooked up a story about an overdue project that needed more library time, and Mom agreed like a lamb.

I did go to the library, actually, and hung around until it closed at nine. I figured it would be safe to take a look at Obelisk by then. There was a separate house on the property for the owner to live in, and I figured Cyrus was bound to be there after hours. Anubis, too. I certainly hoped so—I wasn't keen on meeting *him* in the dark again!

I chained my bike to a streetlight a block away and took the back lane that led past the Obelisk property. I could see lights on in the house, but I decided to check to see if Cyrus was really there. I pussyfooted around to the side of the building. The kitchen light was on, but the room was empty. I prowled a little farther along and peeked in another window.

Bingo!

It looked like a study or library with lots of books lining the walls. A fire was burning in the fireplace, and beside it in a wing chair sat Cyrus. He was naked to the waist and seemed to be wearing some kind of diaper. Or white linen shorts or something. And he had a major amount of gold jewellery around his neck and down his arms. I have to admit he looked even better than he did in his suits. My mom would have gone crazy, not to mention the principal.

Cyrus was reading some kind of scroll and sipping something out of a gold-colored goblet. I checked the room pretty carefully, but there was no sign of Anubis. He was probably out roaming around somewhere. The thought made me uneasy, but I wasn't about to give up now.

I decided to take a look at the funeral home itself. Maybe check out the office in case Cyrus had left anything interesting lying around. I passed the big garage doors at the back, trying not to think too much about the fact that this was where they brought in the hearses with the coffins. And the bodies.

I didn't have a clue how I would get in. But when I tried the handle, the back door swung open silently. A dimly lit hall stretched ahead of me. Part way along it, a strange violet light was spilling from an open doorway. I could hear faint music, too. I crept along the passage, staying close to the wall. When I got to the doorway, it took me a minute to get up my nerve to look in. I mean, I wasn't too crazy about seeing a dead person.

What I saw was worse. A guy bending over a coffin, going quietly about some ghastly business or other. Bathed in that strange violet glow, with eerie music wailing in the background. A tall well-built guy dressed in one of those white diaper things.

Not Cyrus. If only it had been! The hair rose on the back of my neck when I realized who it was. Whose head with its pointed muzzle and bat ears was set on the shoulders of that human body. It was Anubis. And what I was looking at was neither animal nor human.

I would have screamed, except my tongue felt like it was stuck to the roof of my mouth. I don't know how I got out of there. It must have been instinct taking over, because my brain sure wasn't working. I found myself outside in the dark lane gasping for breath. I must have been too scared to breathe on the way out.

I made it to my bike and teetered off home. Of course, my parents jumped all over me for staying out late. But I must have looked as sick as I felt, because they let up pretty quickly and sent me to bed.

There was no way I was going to sleep, though. I tossed and turned, but didn't dare close my eyes. I was too scared that the awful form of Anubis would loom up in the dark while I wasn't looking.

What *was* he anyway? I tossed and turned some more, until I heard my parents come upstairs. A little later, their light went out, and I slipped out of bed and booted up my computer. I put a CD-ROM encyclopedia into the drive and looked up Anubis. And there he was. Anubis the jackal. One of the gods of ancient Egypt. His specialty was embalming bodies—making mummies!—and guiding the souls of the dead on their journey to the underworld.

It figured.

The CD-ROM showed two different pictures of Anubis. One

was a statue of a pointy-nosed, bat-eared dog. Okay, jackal. The other made me shudder just looking at it. It was a human body with the jackal's head. The text went on about how the ancient Egyptians meant that as a kind of symbol.

Not! I'd just seen that jackal-headed dude across town in Cyrus's workroom. Doing his thing!

I learned a lot from that CD-ROM. Not that it cheered me up much. You want to know who the big cheese of the ancient Egyptian underworld was? The all-time mega-God of the Dead? A guy named Osiris. Get it?

I didn't, at first. Not until I'd sneaked downstairs and got the Obelisk business card off the mantel where Mom had put it. I took a real close look at it in the dim light from the computer screen. Just like the flyer. The name Obelisk Services and the image of the monument. And right down at the very bottom, the fine print I hadn't bothered to read the first time:

O. Siris, Proprietor

I'd heard it wrong, you see. Siris, not Cyrus. And right underneath the name were the words:

Service in the Ancient Tradition

No kidding.

I had to admire their sense of humor. Even I've never put over a joke as big as that. What a sweet little operation it was, too. Anubis must always sense who's going to check out next. And who knows? Maybe he uses his weird powers to help them along a little! So all O. Siris has to do is get the advertising out in the right places and rake in the bucks. Very simple.

I didn't tell Jeremy anything about it at school the next day, even though he kept bugging me to find out what had happened. I didn't tell anyone else, either, and I don't plan to. I mean, what's the use? Nobody will believe me. Can't you just see the headlines?

"Boy Cries Dog!

"Does His Mummy Know He's Out?"

I'd be a laughing-stock all over town.

Man, do I wish now that I'd listened to old Jeremy and dropped the whole thing way back. But I couldn't. Oh, no, not me. I just had to get to the bottom of it all. Well, I did. And for once the joke's on me.

'Cause now I'm feeling pretty jumpy, you know? Spooked, you might say. Just a glimpse of a pointy-eared dog brings me out in a cold sweat. And I keep imagining, well, all sorts of nasty scenarios. So I get knots in my neck from looking both ways every time I cross a busy street, in case I might get run over. If I see a ladder leaning against a building, I figure someone up there's going to drop something and squash me flatter than Butcher Baker. And, believe me, I take the long way around. Hey, even eating could be deadly—I might choke, after all. So no more scarfing my food down; these days I chew every mouthful about a zillion times. Mom's thrilled. She says I've turned into a perfect gentleman at the table.

But there are only so many precautions you can take, right? So I'm hanging onto my lucky rabbit's foot, but somehow I don't think even that can help me now.

You see, Anubis followed me home from school yesterday.

Trojan • Horse

Kevin was a gamesman. Each week he waited eagerly for the latest issue of *Compute!* to hit the stands. He couldn't have cared less about the competitive pricing of motherboards and buses. That was nerd stuff. What he wanted was the updated list of cool Web sites where he could download new games.

So when he saw Zack rifling through the paper in the school caf at lunchtime, he reached over his shoulder and grabbed it.

"Hey!" Zack yelled.

"Be cool, man," said Kevin, backing away. "I'll give it back. Just need to check the game-site list."

He thumbed quickly to the right page and glanced down the list of sites. Gladiator.com, mayhem.com, dragonduel.com. He'd tried all those. Weren't there any new sites?

Then, just before Zack was able to grab his paper back, he saw it.

The site was called sinistyr.com. The comment beside the URL read, "Definitely for those who think they've played everything."

Hey, that's me! thought Kevin.

He logged onto sinistyr.com right after supper that night. He had homework, but it couldn't hurt just to suss out the new site first, could it?

He went straight to the games directory. Funny, there was only one game listed. What were these guys, a bunch of wusses? But at least it was a game he'd never heard of before. Trojan Horse, it was called. A descriptor beside the title read, "Ultimate thrills. For major players only."

Well, that's more like it! He selected Trojan Horse and hit Download. Even with his state-of-the-art modem it seemed to take an awfully long time for the game file to transfer.

"Kevin!" His dad's voice boomed up from the foot of the stairs. "Are you doing your homework? Or are you playing games again?"

"Just downloading something, Dad," called Kevin

"Well, make it snappy. Or I'll download something on you."

"Yessir." Kevin had long since learned that a crisp answer was the best way to get his dad off his case.

Five minutes later he had the file safe in his games directory. He'd check it out later.

He didn't get to the new game until the next evening. His parents were going out, so he knew he'd have plenty of time to get the feel of Trojan Horse without his dad butting in. He didn't have to worry about his kid sister either. Dell would love to rat on him, of course, but he figured he had enough on her to guarantee her cooperation.

"Now, you kids know where we'll be," his dad said as they were leaving. "Just six miles down the road at the country club."

"The number's written right by the phone," his mom added. "Just in case you need us."

Dell rolled her eyes. "Awww, Mom," she protested. "I'm twelve, for pity's sake, and Kev's fifteen. What do we need you for?"

Their dad looked at their mom and grinned. "Kind of gives you a nice warm feeling of being wanted, doesn't it?" Then he added, "Well, kids, we won't be late. There's a storm watch for later on tonight, and we'll want to beat the dirty weather home."

Just as they were heading out the door, he looked back and said, "Remember, you two, it's a school night. So I expect both of you to tackle your homework. No games, Kevin. I mean it. Not until your homework's done."

"Yessir." Kevin kept his fingers crossed behind his back when he said it.

As soon as the door closed, Dell stuck her tongue out at him. "Yessir, nosir, three bags full," she chanted. "I saw you cross your fingers behind your back."

"So what?" said Kevin. "You plan to spend the evening doing homework?"

Dell giggled. "You've gotta be kidding," she said.

"Likewise," said Kevin. "Well, enjoy. Catch you later."

They turned their backs on each other and marched off in opposite directions. Kevin heard the TV blaring before he reached the top of the stairs.

He booted up the computer and went to the games directory. First he ran an updated virus scan on the new game just in case, but there was nothing wrong with it. The virus software cleared it for use. He flexed his fingers over the computer keyboard. "Okay, baby, let's fly," he muttered and pressed Enter.

The screen went black. Then the title Trojan Horse came up in dark red letters along with a swell of doom-laden music from the speakers. A tiny red logo appeared in the center of the screen and enlarged rapidly. It was shaped like a knight piece from a chess set—the stylized head of a horse. It got bigger fast until the whole screen was blotted out in a wave of red. Then, for a moment, letters appeared in black on the red field. They read, "WELCOME TO THE FUNHOUSE, SUCKER."

"Huh?" said Kevin, but the words had already disappeared.

Then the screen went black again and stayed that way, except for a few odd wavelike lines that pulsed at regular intervals. No sounds came from the speakers except a faint hissing.

"Awww, c'mon baby!" pleaded Kevin. It would be just his luck to download some screwy defective game!

Maybe he should reboot and try again.

Kevin hit the key to bring up the operating system commands, but nothing happened. The strange lines on the screen just went on pulsing. He tried the Cancel key and the Escape key. Nothing worked.

"Rats!" muttered Kevin. The darn game must have messed up his system software. He reached over to turn off the machine. That was hard on the drive when a program was running, but he didn't know what else to do.

It wouldn't turn off. The screen went right on pulsing like before along with that faint hissing sound.

"Man, oh man," Kevin moaned. Now he was for it. If he

wanted to get his computer fixed, he'd have to tell his dad about the problem. And that meant . . . nuts. Now he'd have to do his homework so his dad wouldn't mind his trying out the game! Talk about a bummer!

He went across to his desk, flipped open his math text and settled down with his chin in his hands. Just wait till he got his computer fixed. He'd send the support guys at sinistyr.com an e-mail that would fry them. Maybe he'd even sue!

After just a couple of minutes he could hear Dell calling him from downstairs. Kevin stomped over to the door and poked his head out.

"Yeah? What?" he yelled.

"The TV's gone funny, Kev," she called. "Come take a look."

"If this is some kind of stupid joke . . ." he threatened as he clumped down the stairs. Dell was always playing tricks on him, and he usually fell for them. So he expected to find her grinning when he showed up. But she wasn't. In fact, she looked puzzled.

"I was watching *Beavis and Butthead* reruns," she complained, "and right in the middle, the screen went all funny."

The TV looked the same as the screen on his computer. Just black nothing video with a weird pulse to it. And a hissing on the audio.

"That's strange. My computer's doing the same thing." Kevin thought there was no need to mention the game that had gone wrong. "Let's try the computer in Dad's office," he said.

"He'll kill you," Dell told him in a singsong voice.

"I'm not going to play with it, dummy," he replied. "I just want to see if it's okay."

The big screen of their dad's very expensive machine was turned on. It was black, too. With pulses. And hissing.

"How come Dad left it on?" Kevin wondered.

Dell shrugged. "Who knows? Anyway, what are we going to do now?"

"Well, what *can* we do? Eat some supper and do our homework, I guess. Or you could dig out your *Piggly Wiggly* books if you really want a blast," he added, smirking. Dell hated to be reminded of how addicted to those sappy books she used to be.

She wrinkled her nose. "Very funny!"

"Yeah, well, I'm getting hungry even if you aren't. Let's nuke something for supper. Then we'll hit the homework."

They headed for the kitchen.

Kevin was rooting in the freezer, when Dell said something he couldn't quite hear.

"Huh?" he said, emerging with a box of double cheese and pepperoni pizza.

"I said the lights on the microwave have gone funny. The stove, too." Dell reached for the pizza box, read the label and grunted her approval.

Kevin peered at the lights on the stove and microwave. All the digital time displays read 00.00, just like after a power failure. And they were pulsing.

"That's funny. Maybe we shouldn't . . ." he began.

But Dell had already ripped the pizza out of the box and was popping it into the microwave. It came on before she had a chance to close the door or set the cooking time.

"Ee-yowch!" she yelped and danced back, shaking her hand.

"It zapped me, Kev!"

"Oh, come on. It couldn't have. It can't operate with the door open," said Kevin.

But the microwave was humming even with the door wide open.

Then he noticed that the TV in the wall by the kitchen door was on, too, its screen black and pulsing.

Suddenly, red words appeared on the screen:

"HORSE 1

"OPPONENT 0

"OPPONENT MOVES."

"What does *that* mean?" asked Dell, still nursing her hand.

"Horse!" gasped Kevin. "That's the name of a new game I downloaded. Trojan Horse. I tried to play it, but I couldn't get it to work. But now . . ."

Dell's eyes widened. "You mean it's playing a *game* with us?"

"It can't be! Can it? It . . . it must have escaped from my computer somehow! That's what's screwing up the other computers and the TV. The microwave, too. It must be getting at the computer chips in the appliances."

"In *all* the appliances? B-But what kind of thing could do that?"

"Nothing I've ever heard of. Must be some crazy virus my scan didn't pick up. It must be something electrical that can travel through the house wiring. . . ."

Suddenly, he smacked himself on the forehead and groaned, "Trojan Horse! Oh, man! Now I get it."

Dell stared at him.

"We learned about it in ancient history," he explained. "A story about attackers hidden inside of something that looked like a gift! And . . . and I downloaded the game for free."

Though he didn't mention it to Dell, he was remembering the game descriptor too: "Ultimate thrills." Suddenly, *ultimate* had a nasty ring to it. It sounded like bait put out to attract smartass games players. Like him. A chill worked its way down his spine. What had he got himself and Dell into?

"W-what are we going to do?" Dell's voice sounded a bit wobbly.

"I dunno."

Just then another message popped up on the TV screen.

"OPPONENT MOVE IN DEFAULT. HORSE MOVES."

A bolt of blue electricity from the TV arced right between Kevin and Dell and struck the stove. The two of them hit the floor. Above them, appliances juddered as electric arcs danced between them. The espresso maker shot steam, and the built-in grill on the top of the stove glowed fiery red. The blender ground and gnashed the air as it inched closer and closer to the edge of the counter above their heads.

"We gotta get out of here!" Kevin yelled over the din. On hands and knees, he and Dell scrambled across the kitchen floor and through the door into the living room.

From behind the living room couch Kevin poked his head up and read from the big-screen TV, which was pulsing faster now.

"OPPONENT STILL IN DEFAULT. HORSE ATTACKS."

Electricity hit the table lamp beside him and sizzled down the cord into the wall.

"Close one," muttered Kevin. "I sure hate the way it seems to know where we are. As if it can sense us somehow."

"I'm scared," Dell whimpered. "I'm calling Mom and Dad."
She jumped up and ran for the phone in the hall.

"No, Dell, don't!" Kevin yelled, pounding after her. "Keep away from it. The phone's . . ."

But Dell had already picked up the receiver. "There's a funny hissing sound," she said, looking back at him.

"Drop it!" screamed Kevin, lunging at her. He knocked her across the hall just as a volley of blue sparks shot out of the phone and zapped across to the brass doorknob beside them. "The phone's electric, too," he finished, panting.

The computer screen in the den read

"HORSE 3

"OPPONENT 0"

Then a new message appeared:

"HORSE PROCEEDS TO ADVANCED GAME MODE."

"What does that mean?" asked Dell, looking around warily for any lurking appliances.

Suddenly, the lights went out. They heard a roar from the direction of the kitchen, then the clatter of wheels on parquet.

"Lordy, what next?" moaned Kevin. A moment later, the dim shape of their mom's big battery-run vacuum cleaner shot through the dining-room doorway and bore down on them.

"It's between us and the front door," he yelled. "Quick, up the stairs!"

At the top of the stairs, they paused, panting, while below them the vacuum cleaner snarled and butted the bottom step.

"This is crazy! We've got to get out of here," wailed Dell as she burst into tears.

31

Kevin put his arm around her shoulders. "Aw, don't cry, Dell. We'll get out of this somehow. C'mon, help me think!"

"S-sorry." Dell gulped back her tears. Then she wiped her eyes and nose on the sleeve of her sweater. "Well, the other stairs go down to the kitchen. You know we'd never make it through there." She thought for a moment, then added, "We could climb out a window, though. Your room's closest."

"Are you kidding? My computer would fry us before we got to the window! And I bet the Horse has taken over your computer, too."

"It'll have to be Mom and Dad's room, then. It's the only one without a TV or a computer."

"C'mon," said Kevin, grabbing her arm. They dashed by the open door of Kevin's room, barely escaping before electricity arched from the pulsing computer screen to an electrical plug on the other side of the hall.

"Yikes," said Kevin. "Well, at least your door's closed." They tiptoed past it to their parents' room and peeked around the door, listening. Nothing. No hissing or whining of demented appliances.

"Don't think there's anything here that can hurt us," Kevin said as they started for the window.

"Clock radio!" screamed Dell, shoving him out of the way as electricity leaped wickedly from the radio to the cell phone on top of the dresser. As she ran she scooped up a pillow from a chair and pitched it at the radio, knocking it to the floor. It hit with a satisfying crash.

"Nice shot! C'mon. Out the window!" yelled Kevin, wrenching it open.

They scrambled through and onto the sloping roof of the veranda. There they stood, gasping in the damp night wind.

"Phew!" said Kevin. "That was close!"

Away to the west, lightning flickered in a bank of heavy cloud. Thunder rumbled.

"What are we going to do now?" asked Dell, shivering. "We can't stay up here—it's going to storm."

"I'll shinny partway down the drainpipe. You follow," Kevin told her. "Put your feet on my shoulders."

They moved to the edge of the veranda roof. Kevin stretched out flat and clung to the eaves trough while he tried to wrap his legs around the drainpipe.

"Look out!" shrieked Dell as a jolt of electricity hit him. He fell off the drainpipe and landed with a whoosh among the shrubs growing near the veranda. When he opened his eyes he could see weird blue fire dancing around the eaves trough and crawling down the drainpipe.

"Kev! Are you okay?" Above him, Dell was outlined against the sky, electricity playing close to her feet.

"I guess." Kevin got up, shaking his head clear. His fingers and toes were numb, and he felt dizzy. "Keep away from anything metal, Dell, or the Horse will zap you, too. You're going to have to jump. It's not so far. I'll break your fall. Hurry!"

"I ca-a-an't!" she screamed, but then a tendril of electricity snaked toward her, and she did.

"Whoof!" grunted Kevin as Dell landed on him and sent them both crashing to the ground. They lay there for a moment, stunned. Then Dell rolled off, but it took a minute for Kevin to get his breath back. Since when had his little sister gotten so darn big? Man, what a night! First shocks, then wallops.

"Okay," he wheezed. "We should be safe out here, but just in case, let's head for the garage. I'll drive the 4x4 out to the road."

"Boy-oh-boy, you'll be in big trouble when Dad finds out," warned Dell. Kevin was strictly forbidden to lay a finger on the 4x4 unless his dad was with him.

"Trouble?" smirked Kevin, struggling to his feet again. "We've already *got* major trouble. Why worry about a bit more?"

Dell got halfway up, then grabbed his arm, wincing in pain. "My ankle," she moaned. "I must have twisted it when I landed."

"Put your arm around my shoulder," Kevin said. "C'mon."

They were halfway across the yard when they heard the sound of a motor sputtering to life in the drive shed. Then around the corner of the farmhouse came the ride-on lawn mower, its long-grass blades whirling viciously. They froze for a moment as its evil-looking single headlight plucked them out of the dark.

"God!" muttered Kevin. "It must have been left plugged in for a battery charge. And the Horse got at it through the wires."

"What are we going to do?" whispered Dell. "It's moving awful fast, and my ankle . . ."

"We'll have to split up. I'll distract it. You get to the garage and back the Jeep out."

"But I can't drive!"

"Oh, yes, you can!" said Kevin. "You know where Dad hides the spare set of keys, don't you?" For once her snoopy habits would pay off.

She nodded.

"Get them. Back the Jeep way out into the field. Then wait for me."

"Okay," she whispered.

"Go!" he ordered and sprang into the oncoming headlight of the mower. He hoped Dell had enough sense to stay behind the bushes that led to the garage.

To make sure the mower followed him, he ran straight toward it, then dashed away from Dell. He figured that he was safe from electricity so long as there was nothing metal for it to jump to. So he only had the mower blades to worry about. As if that weren't enough!

The mower slewed around and charged after him. The thing was even faster than he'd realized! He heard the Jeep start up, then saw it back out of the garage and stall. But Dell got it started again and backed it jerkily across the yard and out into the field. Good old Dell!

Now all he had to do was make it to the Jeep before the mower caught him. At the rate it was moving, that didn't seem likely. Unless . . . unless he could slow it down somehow. But how?

With the blades snicking at his heels, he raced around the corner of the tool shed. Some tools were leaning against the outside wall. Was there anything he could grab? Nothing metal—that would give the Horse something to leap to from the mower, and he'd be toast.

He tripped over the main for the irrigation sprayers and the blades nearly got him. Sobbing for breath, he dashed around the shed again. Then suddenly he knew. Water! Water was bad for electricity, wasn't it? Made it short out or something?

He snatched a wooden-handled shovel as he ran, pitching it at the mower, which was churning close behind him. The shovel clanged off its hood, making sparks flare, but the mower did slow for a moment.

That gave him the time he needed. He hit the control for the irrigation sprinklers, knocking it from the Auto Min setting to On Max.

Then he ran for his life.

Over the pounding of his heart, he could hear the *chukka-chukka-chukka* of the big sprinklers starting up. They were powerful and had a long reach, but they swung around slowly. What if they missed the mower?

It didn't bear thinking about. He ran toward the sprinkler nearest the Jeep. The jet of water hit him forcefully and knocked him to his knees for a moment. He was up and running again when the jet struck the mower.

It wasn't enough. The mower moved right through after him.

But he was almost there. And then he heard Dell, bless her, start up the Jeep again. She moved forward to pick him up.

As the Jeep rolled past him, Kevin yanked the door open, hurled himself inside and slammed the door behind him. The mower charged straight at them.

"Turn toward the road!" Kevin yelled.

"I can't!" cried Dell, clinging to the steering wheel. The mower had gotten itself between them and the driveway, hemming them in against the fence near the pasture.

"It's going to ram us! Turn the ignition off!" As Dell obeyed, Kevin yanked on the emergency brake. He grabbed her, and they huddled in the middle of the seat.

"Stay away from the sides of the car!" he warned. The mower rammed them. Instantly, blue fire leaped from it and crawled all over the vehicle. The mower backed off and rammed the car again just as the sprinkler jet hit both vehicles square on. The mower shot a shower of sparks and died.

Dell cheered.

"Opponents 1," yelped Kevin. "Try the ignition, Dell."

The starting motor ground over and over, but the engine wouldn't catch.

"Spark plugs must be soaked," Kevin groaned. "The sprinkler got them, too."

They sat staring through the wet windshield. Across the field, the lights sprang on again in the farmhouse and pulsed evilly. Electricity crawled up and down the satellite receiver tower beside the house. Around them the irrigation sprinklers revolved, shooting huge jets of water in all directions. Everything was drenched, and puddles as big as small ponds were beginning to form.

"I've never seen so much water," said Dell, awestruck. "Dad's going to have a fit!"

"I hit the control pretty hard. Guess I busted it. So the sprinklers are at max. Dad never uses them that way—it wastes too much water." If only that were all he had to explain, thought Kevin.

Thunder crashed over the chatter of the sprinklers as the storm moved in. Trees near the farmhouse bent in the wind, and the sky was livid with lightning.

"I wish Mom and Dad would get home," said Dell, rubbing her hurt ankle. "The storm's almost here, and they said they'd be back before it hit."

"I don't know what we're going to do when they get here," said Kevin. "That Horse thing isn't just going to go away, you know." He could feel Dell shiver beside him.

The storm was right over them now. A flash of lightning struck the woods beyond the south pasture, and more bolts stalked toward them on crooked legs. Then for a bloodcurdling fraction of a second electricity arced *upward* from the satellite tower. The air crackled as it met a downward lightning bolt. The tower toppled, energy leaping across to wreathe the house in pale fire. Thunder crashed. Kevin squeezed his eyes shut, but the afterimage burned behind his eyelids. He and Dell clung together.

Sheets of rain began to fall. Cautiously, Kevin sat up and peered out through the downpour. He froze, staring at the scene before them.

The satellite receiver tower lay across the yard, a mass of twisted wreckage. The satellite dish had smashed the roof of the veranda. The rest of the house was totally dark, and the sprinklers were still.

"Wow, are we still alive?" gasped Dell. "What happened, Kev?" Kneeling, she pressed her nose against the windshield and stared into the darkness.

"Must have been the mother of all lightning bolts," said Kevin. "All that electricity the Horse was throwing around ran up the tower to meet it. Then the lightning knocked down the tower. I bet it went all through the house, too."

"W-what about the Horse?" asked Dell.

"Maybe the lightning got it," said Kevin. "I hope!" He swung the car door open, and the two of them clambered out. They stood in the rain, listening to the last of the storm grumble in the distance. Minutes later, they saw headlights turning in from the road, and their parents' car came splashing up the driveway.

Kevin and Dell hurried toward them, Dell hobbling as she went.

"Sure glad you two are all right!" their dad said, as he and their mom hugged them. "We'd have been home sooner, but the storm caused local flooding, and the bridge over Becker's Creek went out. We had to go the long way around."

Then he took in the wreckage. "Good God! What happened here?" he demanded, turning to Kevin. "What's the Jeep doing in the field? And how come you and your sister aren't in the house?"

"And why are you limping, Dell?" asked their mom. "What's wrong with your ankle?"

Kevin and Dell both began talking at once.

"We . . . we got scared in the house," Dell babbled.

"Because the power went out," Kevin cut in. "And the lightning was striking all around. So I thought we'd be safer in the Jeep, away from all the buildings."

"And I fell and twisted my ankle running out to the garage," added Dell. "And . . ."

"Then the lightning hit the satellite tower," Kevin finished in a rush.

They glanced at each other from the corners of their eyes. It was all true, wasn't it? They were just leaving some stuff out.

"I think the kids were pretty smart," their mom said. "Aren't you proud of them, Ted?"

"Yeah. Sure," their dad said. But his forehead stayed furrowed, as if he felt something was missing, but couldn't figure out what it was.

They had to spend a week in a motel because the wiring and all the appliances in the house were fused, and had to be replaced. Luckily, most of the cost was paid by their insurance, so it didn't take too long for things to get back to normal.

The first night they moved back into the house, Dell crept into Kevin's room. He was lying on his bed, hands behind his head, staring at the ceiling. His new computer was turned off.

Dell flopped down beside him. For a moment she just sat there, frowning. Then she said, "Kev?"

"Uh-huh?"

"We were right not to tell Dad and Mom about the Horse, weren't we?"

"Yeah. I mean, what else could we do? They wouldn't have believed us anyway." He paused for a moment, then added, "Because you know what, Dell?"

"What?"

"That Web site I got Trojan Horse from. Sinistyr.com. It doesn't exist anymore. I can't find it on the Web now—it's just not there. Whatever jokers created the Horse must have moved on. Guess they thought they'd got at enough suckers like me. So I can't prove a thing."

Dell gulped. "Wow, that's weird," she said.

"Yeah. Weird," he agreed.

Dell got up to go, but halfway out the door she looked back. "Are you sure the Horse is dead, Kev?" she asked.

Kevin frowned. *"Pretty* sure," he replied.

Downstairs in the kitchen, the motor of the shiny new fridge cut in. For a moment it ran smoothly. Then it faltered. Inside, the digital temperature display rolled over to oo and began to pulse. The fridge began to run again, but now, ever so softly, it was humming a whiny little tune to itself.

c a l l • m e

Kelly's silver cell phone rang in the middle of the night. Half asleep, she fished around for it and pressed Rec. "'Lo?" she said groggily. No one answered. "Stupid," she muttered and clicked End.

No sooner had she burrowed comfortably into her pillow, than the phone rang again. "Oh, no," she groaned. Her parents would get right on her case if she started getting calls at this time of night. She dragged the phone under the covers and put it to her ear.

This time there was a voice. "Hello?" it asked. "Uh . . . who is this, please?" It was a guy.

Kelly was miffed. "What do you mean, 'Who is this?'" she demanded. Wide awake now, she sat up and checked the digital clock beside the bed. It read 1:45. "Listen," she muttered into the phone, "you're the one who made the call. Who the heck are you? What number do you want? And what do you mean by calling now?"

There was a long pause, and Kelly's finger moved toward the End button. He could be some kind of creep, after all.

"No, wait. Don't hang up!" the caller said, as if he could read her mind. "It's just . . . I wasn't expecting this. I've had trouble getting through, and I don't know who I've connected with."

"That sounds pretty feeble," Kelly shot back. "You've reached 513-7992. That's all I'm going to tell you." He didn't sound dangerous, she reflected. He wasn't panting in her ear or anything. He sounded young and kind of mixed up. "Just say what you have to say, and hang up," she added. "Don't you know it's the middle of the night?"

"Oh, is it? I'm sorry," said the guy. "I *didn't* know."

"What do you mean you didn't know?" Kelly asked. "Are you calling long distance, or are you just spaced out? Look," she went on, "I'm going to hang up now. Don't forget I have to pay for this call, too. G'bye."

"No! Wait! Don't! It was hard enough to get through this time," the caller said quickly. "Look, you won't have to pay. Honest. I promise. It's not . . . not exactly a regular kind of call."

"I won't have to pay?" Kelly settled back on her pillows. "Well, then, what do you want?"

"I . . . I want you to do me a favor."

Kelly bristled. So he was one of *those.* And she'd just begun to think he was okay. "Oh, no, you don't," she snapped. "Not me. You've got the wrong girl. Listen, there are 1-900 numbers creeps like you can call!" She punched End and put the phone back on the bedside table.

A minute later it rang again.

Kelly was really angry now. "Stop bugging me!" she snapped.

"Sorry . . . I'm sorry. But I need to talk to you. This is really important," the guy said. It was the same one, of course. He sounded upset and somehow farther away than the first time.

"Your signal is fading," said Kelly. "Why don't you just give it up?" Then, "Hey, this isn't some kind of emergency call, is it?" she asked, suddenly worried.

"Sort of," he said.

"What do you mean, 'Sort of'?"

"Well, it's not me who's in trouble. But someone is. That's why I need you to do me the favor."

Kelly sighed. There was obviously no way she was going to get rid of him until she heard him out. "Okay," she said. "Tell me what the favor is."

"I need you to take a message to someone," came the answer.

"Why don't you just phone whoever it is yourself?" she asked.

"I can't get through. I've tried and tried. You're the only person I've been able to reach," the guy said.

"So, go over and see whoever it is."

The caller sighed. "I can't," he said. "It's against the rules around here. I guess doing this is, too, but they haven't stopped me yet."

Uh-oh, Kelly told herself. This is beginning to sound weird. "Now, look, whoever you are . . ." she began.

"My name's Charley," he said quickly. "What's your name?"

"Sorry, Charley," Kelly said. "There's no way I'm going to tell you that."

"Oh," he said. Then, "Yeah, I guess I can understand why. I mean, I could be anyone, couldn't I?"

"As far as I'm concerned you *are* just anyone," said Kelly.

"Calling me in the middle of the night. Asking me for favors. Is that weird or what?"

There was a long pause. Then Charley said softly, "You're right. But you see, I just don't know what else to do. The poor kid needs help. I've tried every way I can think of to get through to her, but I can't. Then, just when I'd given up, this . . . this connection happened."

Kelly felt a twinge of sympathy. It was a young girl he wanted to get the message to. The guy sounded pretty unhappy. It didn't seem right just to hang up on him. "Look," she said at last. "Here's what I'll do. You tell me the message and the phone number of the person, and I'll phone her. I could tell her to call you."

"No, that wouldn't work," said Charley.

"Well, then, I'll send the message in a letter. I'll even pay for the stamp," Kelly added with a burst of generosity. "How's that?"

"No. I'm sorry, but no. Someone has to tell her. In person. You have to go yourself."

That was too much for Kelly. "Well, that's my final offer. Now, goodnight, and please don't call me back. I'm turning the phone off now."

She did. But it took a long time for her to get to sleep.

The next day at school she told her friend Cheryl all about it during lunch. She had her cell phone with her, and she pulled it out and put it on the table. Exhibit A.

"Wow!" breathed Cheryl when she'd heard the story. "Did he sound like a sex fiend, or what?" She kept nibbling on her slice of pizza, but her eyes were as big as CDs.

Kelly shook her head slowly. It was fun to have Cheryl hang-

ing on her every word. Usually *she* was the one with exciting
things to tell. She took a large bite of her sandwich, chewed, and
swallowed before she answered. "Nope. He sounded kind of
nice, actually. But worried . . . about this girl he needs to get
through to."

"Not a fiend, huh?" Cheryl sounded a little disappointed. She
dabbed daintily with a paper napkin at a splotch of tomato sauce
on her chin.

"I sure didn't get that feeling," said Kelly. "I mean, when he
went, 'I want you to do me a favor,' I thought, Whoaa, here we
go. But then . . . No, I don't think he's kinky, whatever he is."

Cheryl narrowed her eyes the way she always did when she was
concentrating. She took a sip of her Coke, then almost choked
as she thought of something. "I've got it!" she spluttered.
"Absolutely for certain sure!"

"What?" Kelly eyed her warily. Cheryl was always coming up
with weird ideas, probably because she watched so many soaps.

"The guy's in jail, that's what," said Cheryl. "Look, it fits, does-
n't it? He says he can't do stuff because the rules don't allow it. This
girl he's involved with is unhappy, but he can't see her or phone her.
Then he somehow gets his hands on a cell phone and . . ."

"Calls *me*," Kelly finished sarcastically. "Oh, sure. Why would
he do that?"

"Well, why not?" said Cheryl eagerly. "Just by accident, he got
you. Maybe he just couldn't get through to his girl for some reason."

"He did say he'd tried and tried," Kelly reflected.

"Well, there you are. Kind of romantic, isn't it?" Cheryl extended
her hand, palm upward, under Kelly's nose. "Madame Cherylazunga

sees all, knows all, tells all. Cross my palm with silver?"

"Get serious!" snorted Kelly. But her head was full of jail images as they got up. A pale face behind bars. A lonely figure in a dark cell. Maybe Cheryl had something after all.

"Just remember," Cheryl said as they dumped their trays and headed for their next class. "In case I'm wrong, I mean. If he turns out *not* to be in jail and tries to get you to meet him somewhere, don't do it."

"C'mon, I'm not that dumb!" protested Kelly.

"Yeah, well, some of those guys can be pretty convincing. And then . . . bingo!"

"Bingo?"

"You know what I mean," warned Cheryl, rolling her eyes.

"He really didn't sound that bad," said Kelly. Then she wondered why she was defending a weirdo like Charley. It was just something about the way he talked to her. Sincere. Yeah, that was it. "Anyway," she added, "I'm pretty sure I won't hear from him again. 'Cause I told him I wouldn't deliver the message."

The phone rang again late that afternoon. Kelly had left her cell phone upstairs and had to dash to pick it up.

"Hi, Mom. It's Kelly," she said breathlessly. It was about the time of day her mother called to see if Kelly had given her little sister, Chloë, an after-school snack and if Kelly was doing her homework.

"Hi. Uh, Kelly?" said Charley's voice. "Is this a better time for you? I thought I'd better wait a long while before I tried calling you again."

Kelly sat down suddenly on the edge of her bed. Rats. Now

she'd given her name away to him! "It's you," she said. "Yes, of course, it's better. At least it's not the middle of the night."

"That's good," came the reply. "It's kind of hard to tell here, you see."

Wow, Cheryl's right! thought Kelly. They've got him in solitary confinement. With the lights out. He must have done something awful! She was dying to ask him what.

"Look," she said. "I still don't want to deliver your message. And I won't meet you anywhere either, so there!"

To her surprise, Charley laughed. "I can't meet you either, Kelly. So we're even on that one."

Definitely jail, thought Kelly. "Well," she said.

"Well," he repeated. Then he said hopefully. "It's a very short message, Kelly."

Kelly groaned and flopped back on the bed. "Look, Charley, it doesn't matter how long or short the message is. I just can't get involved. It's not as if it's a life-or-death emergency or something. I mean, is it?"

There was a long pause. Then Charley said, "No, not life or death exactly. More like . . . how someone's going to feel about her life."

"Huh?"

He sighed. "Look. There's someone who doesn't like herself anymore. Who's miserable because of a stupid fight we had. . . ."

Kelly sat up. "This girl, you mean? Whoever she is? You had a quarrel and . . ."

"Yes." His voice seemed to be getting fainter again.

"Hey, Charley, I'm losing you," said Kelly. "Charley?"

There was no one there.

"Drat!" said Kelly. She punched End and sat cross-legged on the bed, the phone cradled in her lap. Just when it was getting interesting! Cheryl was right—it *was* kind of romantic. This guy, whatever he'd done, and his girl. They'd had a fight and he'd gone off and done something stupid and got himself put in jail. And now the girl blamed herself. She was miserable, he'd said. Well, of course she would be. Kelly knew *she* would be miserable if it had happened to her boyfriend. Well, she would be if she had a boyfriend, she corrected herself.

She chewed on the end of a strand of hair to help her think. It wouldn't really be so wrong to help him, would it? Just go over to the girl's place and deliver a message that would make things better for her? It would be doing a kindness really. Besides, she had to admit she was longing to see her. Kelly could almost imagine what the girl would look like. She'd be dressed in black, and her face would be beautiful, but pale and sad. Then it would light up with joy when Kelly mentioned Charley's name. . . .

I'd be a hero, sort of, Kelly thought. She looked down at the phone, willing it to ring. But it didn't.

"Well? Did he call you again?" Cheryl asked eagerly the next day. "Uh-huh."

"And you're going to do it, aren't you?"

Kelly nodded.

"I *knew* it!" Cheryl pumped her fist in the air. "Stray-K rules! The softest center since Caramilk!"

Kelly made a face. She'd never live down that stupid nickname. Kids began calling her that back in elementary school because stray animals always seemed to find their way to her. At one point in her life, she'd had three cats and a dog that she'd got that way, and she would have had more if her mother hadn't put her foot down.

"Anyway," she said, "I won't do it if the message is anything gross."

"Well, yeah, naturally," agreed Cheryl.

She was really into this thing all the way, Kelly could see that. Actually, it was kind of neat to be the daring one for once.

"Uh . . . I could come with you," Cheryl offered.

"Thanks, but, you know, two might be a crowd or something," Kelly said loftily. "It's pretty delicate, after all. I don't think Charley would like more people hanging around. I mean, this girl is clearly the love of his life, and she's feeling bad."

"I guess you're right," Cheryl sighed as she pulled books out of her locker. "You're a lucky duck, though, Kelly. I wish he'd called *me*. Doesn't it sound like something out of a romance novel?" she went on dreamily. "Or out of one of those oldie movies? A silly quarrel, lovers separated by fate . . ."

Kelly slung her backpack over one shoulder and slammed her locker door. "Well, no use getting ourselves all worked up," she said. "I didn't tell him I'd do it for sure. And he mightn't even be able to call me back. There's something really wrong with the signal—he just keeps fading away."

But Charley called again the very next day. This time Kelly was ready and waiting, sitting in her bedroom with the phone right in front of her. She'd figured that if he did call it might be in the late afternoon again.

She pounced on the phone after the first ring. "Charley?" she said eagerly.

"Uh, yeah. Kelly? Sorry to keep bugging you. But . . . it's . . . I really can't explain it. You seem to be the only person I can get through to somehow."

"Is she . . . that girl . . . is she still upset?"

"Yeah. She's feeling real bad. I've got to help her—I've just got to."

There was a quiver in his voice that turned Kelly's heart to mush. It's true love, all right, she told herself. Aloud, she said, "Uh, Charley? What's the message?"

His voice leaped with hope. "You'll do it?" he gasped. "You'll go and tell her the message?"

"Tell it to me first," bargained Kelly. "Then I'll decide."

"Okay," he said quickly. "All you have to say when you see her is, 'No sweat, Mouse.'"

No-sweat mouse? What kind of love message was that? And what the heck was a no-sweat mouse anyway? "That's it?" Kelly asked, puzzled.

"That's it. She'll understand."

"You're sure she won't be, like, uh, kind of disappointed?"

"Nope."

Well, thought Kelly, it takes all kinds. Maybe it was some kind of secret code or something. Anyway, there was nothing wrong with the message as far as she could see.

"Okay, I'll do it," she agreed. "How do I find her?"

"Gee, Kelly, will you really? That's great. Her name is Maggie. I mean, Margaret. Margaret Cortland. She lives at 31 Elm. Apartment 203."

"That's way across town. I'll have to take a bus . . ." Kelly glanced at her watch. It was just after four. "I could go over right now. Would she be home?"

"Oh, yes," said Charley. Then, as his voice grew fainter, "Oops, I'm starting to fade again. Thanks, Kelly. Thanks a million!"

"Will you call back . . . ?" Kelly started to ask, but the connection was gone.

She thought she'd better call Maggie's place before going over, so they'd be expecting her. There was just one Cortland on Elm Street in the phone book, so she dialed the number.

A man's voice answered.

"Uh . . . hello," said Kelly. "My name is Kelly Kolchak. I was wondering, I mean, I've got a message from Charley. . . ."

As soon as she said the name, the man at the other end drew in his breath. Then he slammed down the receiver.

Whoaa! Kelly said to herself, dropping the phone on the bed as if it had singed her fingers. Guess they don't like Charley much. She sat with her chin in her hands, considering. It made sense, come to think of it. If *she'd* gotten involved with a guy who ended up in jail, her parents wouldn't be too thrilled either.

For a moment she thought of giving it up. She sure wasn't eager to meet the guy who'd hung up on her. But she thought about Charley and began to feel guilty. It would be cowardly to back out now. She'd just have to go over to Elm and try to see Maggie-Margaret in person. After all, she'd promised Charley. She at least had to try.

Kelly caught a bus across town and transferred to another. It took only a few minutes to walk over to Elm from the bus stop, and number 31 was just a couple of blocks down. Kelly glanced at her reflection in the window of a shop as she passed. She looked okay. She'd even changed her sweats and jeans for a skirt and sweater. After the way her call had been received, she figured they mightn't be all that glad to see her. Except Maggie, of course.

It wasn't the sort of place that had a security system. Kelly just took the elevator up to the second floor and knocked on the door of number 203.

A woman answered. Kelly noticed that she looked pale and tired, as if she'd been ill.

Clearly puzzled, the woman looked her up and down. "Yes?" she asked.

"Uh, hi. I'm Kelly Kolchak."

"Are . . . are you a friend of Charley's?" the woman asked. She tried to smile, but it kept slipping away.

Kelly was surprised. Charley? But this was supposed to be Maggie's place. "Well, sort of. Not exactly. We've talked on the phone sometimes."

"I don't remember his mentioning your name. But thank-you for coming." The woman stepped aside and gestured for Kelly to come in.

The living room was on the shabby side, but very, very neat.

"I really came to see Maggie," Kelly explained. "I have a message for her."

"Margaret? She's in her room. Please sit down, and I'll call her." The woman turned, went down the hall and rapped softly on a door. "Maggie? There's someone here to see you, dear."

A large rumpled-looking man with a coffee mug came into

the living room from the kitchen. He stopped, surprised, when he saw Kelly perched on the edge of the sofa.

It must be the guy she'd talked to on the phone, thought Kelly, getting up. The unfriendly one. "H-hello. I'm Kelly Kolchak," she ventured.

His eyebrows drew together into a solid black line. "Kelly Kolchak? Weren't you the one on the phone a while back?" he demanded.

Kelly nodded, not daring to say anything more.

"Kelly's a friend of Charley's, Jim," the woman said, returning to the living room. "She's come to see Maggie. But, Kelly, I don't know whether she'll talk to you. She's been so upset since . . . since it happened. She has hardly eaten or slept." She pulled a tissue out of her sleeve and dabbed at her eyes.

Well, that figures, Kelly thought to herself. Charley had told her that Maggie was terribly upset. But she wasn't sure what to do if Maggie didn't want to talk to her. She couldn't very well barge into the girl's room and insist! Anyway, the big guy wouldn't let her. She was sure of that.

Then a little girl no older than seven or eight came down the hall. She went over to Kelly and gazed up at her.

"*You're* Maggie?" Kelly asked, stunned. Where was the romantic young woman she'd been expecting to meet?

The little girl was plain and pale, and her mouse-blonde hair hung about her thin face in wisps. There were huge dark circles under her eyes. Kelly thought she'd never seen such a sad face in her life.

The woman put her arm around the girl's shoulder and said, "Maggie, this is Kelly Kolchak. She's a friend of Charley's. Isn't it kind of her to come and see us?"

At the mention of Charley's name, Kelly saw a flicker of pain in Maggie's eyes, but she said nothing.

What do I do now? thought Kelly desperately. She decided she'd better charge ahead. "Uh, Maggie," she began hesitantly, "I've got a message for you. From Charley."

Maggie's eyes widened, but before she could say anything, the man burst in.

"How dare you say you have a message from Charley?" he growled. "Are you some kind of nut case?" He glared at Kelly, who took a step back.

"Please, I . . . don't know what's the matter," she quavered. "Charley asked me to deliver a message to Maggie. He said it was important."

"You're lying," the man said bitterly. "Unless . . . when did Charley ask you to do this?"

"About an hour ago," said Kelly, biting her lips. She was feeling really frightened. Nothing was turning out the way she'd thought it would!

"That's impossible!" Picking up a folded newspaper from the coffee table, he shook it under Kelly's nose. "Read the date on this paper, young lady! Read the headline!"

Kelly took the paper with trembling fingers and read the date. It was from four days earlier. Then she read the headline: "Tragic Death of Local Youth." She swallowed and kept on reading.

One of the city's most promising high school basketball players died suddenly yesterday during a game against

Forest Park Collegiate. Charles Cortland collapsed during the game and was rushed to Centennial Hospital, where he was pronounced dead on arrival. Doctors believe his death was due to an aneurysm in the brain. . . .

Charley was dead—he had been dead for five days!

"No," whispered Kelly, shaking her head. "No, it can't be!"

The man just stood there glowering at her, but the woman said, "You understand now, don't you? It couldn't have been our Charley who gave you a message today, Kelly. It couldn't have been. You must have made a mistake. Or . . . or you're trying to play a cruel joke on us."

"A joke?" gasped Kelly. What kind of monster would do a thing like that? She dropped the paper and backed toward the door. "No, I'd never do such a mean thing. Honest!"

"Kelly, wait!" cried Maggie. She ran over and grabbed Kelly's hand.

"Maggie . . ." the man began. But the woman shook her head at him and he fell silent.

Still clutching Kelly's hand, Maggie led her down the hall to a closed door. She turned the handle and the door swung open on a cheerful messy room hung with pennants and decorated with shelves of trophies. A basketball sat forlornly in the only chair.

Maggie turned and looked up at Kelly. "This is Charley's room," she said gravely. "It's just the way it was before . . . before . . ."

"Before he died?" asked Kelly in a small voice.

Maggie nodded. "It's all my fault," she said. Her voice caught and broke. *"They* don't know about it, or they wouldn't go on being nice to me," she said nodding toward the living room. "They'd hate me if they knew. But it's true."

"Maggie, you're wrong!" cried Kelly. "It said right in the paper. Charley died because of a . . . well, something that burst in his brain. Because of the game. It had nothing to do with you!"

"Oh, yes, it did," Maggie insisted, nodding wisely. "Charley was always teasing me, you know. And I'd get mad at him and then we'd fight. That's what happened that day. And I got really mad and told him I hated him." She shivered and then struggled on, "And . . . and . . . I told him I wished he'd drop dead. And he did. So you see it *is* my fault." She stared up at Kelly with solemn eyes.

Kelly dropped to her knees and put her hands on Maggie's shoulders. "Maggie, honey, listen to me. It wasn't your fault. Believe me. Charley doesn't think so. He loves you. I . . . I don't know how this can be—I mean, it's kind of like a miracle—but . . . but I spoke with Charley just a little while ago. He sent me here today to tell you something. I don't understand the words, but he said you would. Maggie, he said to tell you, 'No-sweat mouse.'"

"No sweat, Mouse?" Maggie repeated. "He really said that?" She began to tremble, and her eyes brimmed over with tears. "He called me Mouse," she whispered. "He always did. Because of my mousy hair. And when we'd fight and then make up, that's what he'd say. It meant that our fight didn't matter. That he loved me."

"No sweat, Mouse," Kelly said slowly. "Now I get it. So you

see, don't you? He's telling you it's okay. It wasn't your fault, and he doesn't want you to blame yourself."

"Yes," said Maggie. Then, with a great sob, "Oh, Charley!" She threw her arms around Kelly's neck and began to cry.

Kelly sat on the back porch steps with her cell phone beside her. She wrapped her arms around her knees and watched the stars come out. It was getting late. She'd have to go in soon.

Would Charley even know she'd done what he asked?

The phone rang, and she snatched it up.

"H-hello?" she gasped.

"Kelly?" His voice sounded faint, as if he were farther away than he'd ever been before.

"Charley!"

"Thanks, Kelly," he said. "Maggie will be okay now."

"Charley, where are you? How can I be talking to you?"

He chuckled. "It's pretty hard to explain. I guess this sort of thing doesn't happen very often. It's against all the rules. But once in a while . . ."

His voice died away.

"Wait! Don't go yet," she cried. "Charley, are . . . are you some kind of ghost? Or . . . ?" But he was gone. With a shivery sigh, Kelly hugged the cell phone to her chest. Imagining white robes. Imagining wings.

T H E • V I L L A G E

A ndrew clumped up the basement stairs, his arms full
of the battered cardboard boxes that contained the
Christmas village. His sister, Madeleine, who was
passing through the hall, peered down the stairs at him, then
raised her voice in a wail of protest. "Andrew! You're not putting
up that ugly old thing again. Mother! Tell him he can't!"

Their mother was addressing Christmas cards at a desk in the
den across the hall. As Andrew went by, heading for the living
room, she glanced up at him over the tops of her half-moon
reading glasses. She shrugged and turned back to her task. "Oh,
let him be, Maddy," she said when Maddy stuck her head in the
door. "You know how fond he's always been of the village."

"But he's going to take down my mantel decorations—it'll
spoil everything!" Maddy complained. "I've done the mantel and
the tree all in silver with blue velvet bows to match the carpet. It
looks heavenly. That fusty old village will spoil everything!"

"Now, Maddy," their mother said. "That fusty old village, as you
call it, belonged to my parents. I remember loving it myself as a child."

"Fine," said Maddy. "But Andrew's not a child anymore. He's

fourteen. He only wants to put the village up because he knows it bugs me."

Ignoring the fuss his sister was making, Andrew set the boxes down on the living-room coffee table and began removing her decorations from the mantel. To him, it was perfectly simple. No village, no Christmas. And no amount of silver tinsel and blue velvet was going to change his mind.

Maddy hadn't given up. She followed him into the living room. "You're just being stubborn, Andrew. You're too old to really care about that old village anymore. Look at Bella. She's only seven, and she doesn't care beans about it. Do you, Bella?"

Their little sister was sitting cross-legged on the carpet near the mantel, her curly blonde head bent over a coloring book. She glanced up as she chose another marker. "Nope. But Andrew does," she said simply. "So you just leave him alone, Maddy."

Andrew reached down and ruffled her hair. "Thanks, Bellaphant," he said. It was his old nickname for her.

She grinned up at him, then returned to her coloring.

"Well, all right," snapped Maddy. "But don't blame me if people think we're weird and tacky having this dirty old stuff around!" She flounced out of the living room, and her feet beat an angry patter up the stairs to her room. A door slammed loudly.

Their mother got up and came into the living room to look at the village. Andrew had unrolled a piece of cotton batting along the length of the mantel. That was the snow. Now he was unpacking the houses that would line the village street.

"Oh, dear. They *are* getting awfully shabby, aren't they?" his mother said, touching one of the houses with the tip of a finger. "If only they'd been made out of wood instead of cardboard. They'd have lasted much longer."

"I like them the way they are," said Andrew.

"You would, you old stick-in-the-mud," said his mother, smiling. "I've never known anyone who liked things to stay the same as much as you do. But I really think this will have to be the last year you put the village up. It's getting to be an eyesore."

"Grandpa and Grandma liked it," Andrew pointed out.

"Well, so did I, when I was little. It was in better shape then, and in their old-fashioned house it looked as if it belonged," she replied. "But here . . ." She glanced around the elegant living room, with its pale furniture and blue carpet so thick that people's shoes left imprints in it, and shook her head.

"But I promised Grandma I'd always put it up!" Andrew knew it had been a childish promise, but it still meant a lot to him.

His mother's eyes softened. "I know you did. And I know how much you loved your grandpa and grandma. But not all promises are forever, are they?" she asked. "Anyway, I'm afraid Maddy has a point. Don't you think you're too old to make such a fuss about this, Andrew?" When he didn't reply, she shrugged and went back to the den.

Andrew sighed. Of course, they all thought he was just being childish. Or stubborn. Maybe he was. But the Christmas village had been part of his grandparents' house. His visits there at Christmas and during the summer holidays had been the happiest times of his life. Over the years, though, his family's visits had become fewer because they had moved farther and farther away.

Then his grandfather had died and his grandmother had had to sell the house and move into a retirement home. Not long afterward, she too died.

For Andrew, that had been like the closing of a door into a world he'd always loved and yearned for. Even if someone had bothered to ask, he couldn't have explained why he felt that way, so perhaps it was just as well that nobody ever did.

It was something to do with . . . with *wholeness,* he told himself now, groping for the right word. The village where his grandparents had lived had been somewhere in itself, not just a piece of a bigger place. People had been part of it all. He could remember summer evenings at his grandparents' house, with crickets chirping in the long grass and fireflies winking among the bushes in his grandmother's big overgrown garden. All along the street, people would be sitting out on their verandas, talking softly and calling, "Good evening," when neighbors walked by. Everyone knew everybody else, and they all fitted together like the pieces of the big jigsaw puzzles his grandmother always set up on a card table in a corner of the porch.

Christmas was even better. There was always snow, tons of it, shoveled into shining mounds along the paths, weighing down the branches of the big balsam firs around the house. People would go tobogganing on Spillman's Hill just outside town. The little pond at the end of the street would freeze and there'd be skating. Every house would have a real Christmas tree—green and spicy-smelling—standing inside the front window, and people would visit each other, bundled up against the cold and calling greetings through the frosty air.

Summer or winter, the village was simply there for Andrew in a way that no other place could be. His grandparents had told so many stories about it way back to their own childhoods and beyond that he felt as if he were part of their olden days himself.

Despite his mother's urging, her parents had refused to give up their big house in the village. "There have always been Butlers here," his grandfather used to say. "Always have been, always will be."

Grandpa had been wrong about that, thought Andrew. There were no Butlers left there anymore. Even the village itself had changed. Well before his grandmother sold the house, the village had become surrounded by housing estates, the fields and woods around it dug up like giant molehills, the narrow main street choked with traffic. There would be no use going back there now, even if he could.

All he had left of that lost world was the Christmas village. Year in, year out, it had stood on his grandparents' mantel all through December. When his grandmother sold the house, she had it packed up and waiting for them.

"You'd better take it, Jo," she'd told their mother. "I'll have no place to put it up where I'm going—no fireplace, no mantel." She'd made a wry face.

"Oh, Mother, it's getting pretty battered," their mother protested.

But Andrew had spoken up quickly. "It's wonderful, Grandma. I'll take good care of it and put it up every Christmas," he'd promised. And he always had.

Andrew went on unwrapping houses now and placing them carefully along the mantel. His favorite, the steepled church, he placed in the middle, with all the other buildings lined up on either side. The grandest house was a big Victorian mansion, with verandas and a tower. Next to it went a brick saltbox with a sloping back roof and then a smaller gray cottage with its own wishing well. On the other side of the church went another square brick house and then the village inn with its big windows. At the very end of the street, he put the covered bridge.

He fitted a string of lights so that each little house would be lit by a bulb within. Then he dug in the bottom of the box for smaller objects wrapped in tissue. Out came pointed pine trees made of porcelain, their ragged tiers dusted with snow, and bare-limbed oaks, each with tiny cardinals and bluejays perched on its branches.

Last came the people. They, too, were made of porcelain. Andrew could remember his grandfather lifting him up to look at them when he was small, and he knew even then that they were special, not toys to be played with.

Andrew unwrapped them carefully and put them in their places. His grandfather had jokingly named them for real neighbors who had lived in the village when he was young. Here was Kate Gray, his favorite, with her long yellow hair escaping from her blue hood. She was pulling a sled with her rosy-cheeked little brother, Billy, on it.

At one end of the street, there was space in the cotton batting for a bit of mirror, and there Andrew set up the skating pond, placing two brown-haired boys in toques and mufflers so that their tiny silver skates seemed to glide over the mirror's surface. These were John and Thomas, Kate's older brothers. The figures were laughing as if they were having a good time, Andrew thought, remembering the skating on the village pond when he was little. Of course, he could go skating at the arena here in town any time he wanted. But it wasn't the same.

At the other end of the little street, just coming out of the covered bridge, he placed a one-horse sleigh driven by a man in a cap with earflaps. That was Doc Gray, Kate's father. Andrew's grandfather had said he was always about at all hours delivering babies. And outside the church he put two ladies with long skirts and fur-trimmed jackets—Mrs. Carson, the schoolteacher, and Miss Albright, who ran the village grocery shop. Last of all, down by the little gray cottage, he set grumpy-looking Mr. Edwards. Gray-haired and bent, he was dragging his Christmas tree home through the snow.

Andrew plugged in the string of lights behind the village houses and switched the room lights off. It was always a magic moment when the little street sprang to life. When he was small he'd pretended there were other people behind the lighted windows of the houses, laughing and preparing for Christmas.

"Hey!" protested Bella. "I can't color in the dark!"

"You still there, Bellaphant?" he asked. "Sorry. I just wanted to see the village lit up."

She got up and stood beside him, gazing at it.

"It looks good now, doesn't it, Bella?" Andrew asked. "Now it's dark and you can see the lights."

"I guess," said Bella, doubtfully. "Maddy doesn't like it, though."

"No," agreed Andrew. "She sure doesn't!"

The front door burst open, letting in a gust of cold air and a swirl of snowflakes. "Hey, Andrew, Bella—what's all this dark and gloom?" their father demanded, stamping his feet and brushing snow off his broad shoulders. He reached for the switch in the hall, and suddenly the room blazed with light again. "Where is everyone?" he called. "Family conference time! Where's Maddy? Where's Pete?"

Their mother came out of the den and kissed him. "Maddy's upstairs. Sulking, I suppose. Pete's not home yet—he had basketball practice."

Their father stood rubbing his hands together. He was a big Viking of a man with blond hair and a ruddy complexion. "Cold as Siberia out there," he said grinning. "But we won't have to worry about that for long."

"What are you talking about?" their mother asked.

"Oh, nothing. Nothing at all. Just the biggest best Christmas surprise this family's ever had," he said cheerfully.

"A surprise!" yelped Bella. Trampling her markers underfoot, she dashed over to her father. "What is it, Daddy?" she wheedled, grabbing his hands. "Tell us."

"Nope," he said, picking her up and swinging her around. "Not a peep out of me till Pete and Maddy get here."

"Oh, don't be such a tease, Maurice," said their mother. Then the back door slammed. "There. I think I hear Pete now." She turned and called, "Is that you, Pete? Come along to the living room, please." She went to the foot of the stairs and called up, "Maddy? Come down. Dad has something to tell us."

In a moment, they were all there, jostling each other cheerfully. Pushing out the walls, Andrew thought. He'd never seen a room yet that his big golden family hadn't made seem small.

Their father came over to stand in front of the fireplace. He gave Andrew a playful punch on the shoulder. "How's it going, son?" he asked.

"Okay, Dad," said Andrew. "I just set up the Christmas village."

"What, that old thing again?" his father asked, raising his eyebrows.

"I told him, Dad!" Maddy chimed in. "I did a gorgeous mantel decoration, and he went and took it down,"

"So what?" returned Andrew. "Nobody asked you to decorate the mantel. I always put up the village. Always!"

"Well, we won't need to bother about it anymore," their father cut in. "Now, pipe down, both of you," he went on. "Here I've come home with a great piece of news, and you're so busy arguing that nobody wants to hear it!"

"I do, I do!" cried Bella, hopping from one foot to the other.

"Me, too, Dad," agreed Pete. "So spill."

"Well, then." Their father stuck his hands in his pockets and looked from one expectant face to the next for dramatic effect. "What would you all say if I told you we're moving to Florida?"

"Florida!" their mother gasped. "But Maurice, we've only lived here a year. We've hardly begun paying for the house!"

Their father grinned. "Yep! But this family is always on the move. Upward. Always upward!"

"But . . . Florida?"

"That's in the States!" exclaimed Maddy.

"Right." Their father sat down on the sofa, pulling their mother down beside him and putting his arm around her. "They're making me vice-president of production for all of North America. So I have to be at head office. And that's in Florida. Tampa, to be exact. And don't worry, Jo. With what I'll be getting paid from now on we can afford a house that's a palace compared to this!"

There was a moment's silence.

"Well, aren't you all thrilled?" Their father sounded disappointed.

"Thrilled!" yelped Maddy. "What about my boyfriend?"

"Now, come on, Princess," her father said, winking at her. "A gorgeous girl like you won't have any trouble finding dozens of boyfriends. Those American boys will fall at your feet—take it from me."

"It's wonderful about your promotion," their mother began. "It's everything we've dreamed of, hoped for. But what about me? I guess I could wind things up here fairly soon, but I'd have to requalify there before I could practice."

Andrew could see her mind at work as she spoke, already figuring out the best way to go about it.

"What about my basketball?" Pete wanted to know.

"More and better!" their father promised. "And year-round tennis outdoors. Football. All the stuff you like. Plus water-skiing and scuba-diving."

"And me, Dad?" Bella wanted to know. "What will there be for me?"

Their father beckoned her over. Then he leaned down and put

his mouth close to her ear. "Alligators," he hissed.

"Real live ones? Wow! Just wait till I tell the kids at school," Bella said gleefully.

"But when do we actually have to leave, Maurice?" asked their mother. "I can't possibly go this month. I'm still in the middle of the Larkin case, remember."

"Don't worry. We won't have to leave until well into the New Year. Late January—or maybe February. Well, I'll probably have to go down for a while right after Christmas."

"January!" screeched Maddy, racing for the stairs. "I've got to phone Tim. And Leslie and Amber."

"That's still not much time," their mother murmured, half to herself.

Abuzz with their plans, the rest of the family drifted off toward the kitchen.

Andrew stayed behind. Florida! he thought numbly. How was he going to live in Florida? It was flat, wasn't it? No trees. Well, maybe palm trees, like dried-up sticks with mops stuck on top. No snow, for sure. Warm weather all the time. His dad was right. Pete and the others would probably like it. But he knew he wouldn't. He liked living where the seasons changed and the winters were snowy.

"I can't go," he whispered, watching the snow fall outside the window. "I just can't!"

If only his grandparents were still alive, he could go and live with them. They'd have taken him, he knew. It was a family joke, how much he was like his quiet dark-haired grandfather and how little like his own noisy family.

"My changeling child," his mother sometimes called him. Once she said to Pete, "If Andrew didn't look so much like your grandpa, I'd swear he'd got switched with some other baby at birth."

"Hey, great idea, Mom. Let's advertise," Pete had joked. "Maybe some dark-haired folks out there have a big blond kid they can't figure out. We could swap!" He'd given Andrew a friendly cuff to show he didn't mean it.

But Andrew knew that in a way Pete was right. He didn't belong, not really. He wasn't popular like Maddy or good at sports like Pete. Or lively and clever like Bella. He was just . . . ordinary. Even his name was plain. He liked Andrew best, not a nickname.

And now Florida. He'd have to start over again. They all would, but he knew his brother and sisters would soon fit in. They always did. For him, though, it would be different. Every time they'd moved, which had been often, it had been like trying to grow new skin over a wound. And now it would be the same thing all over again.

"I *won't* go," he said under his breath.

He turned back to the village. There'd be no place for that in Florida, for sure. There probably wouldn't even be a mantel. What would people in a hot climate want with fireplaces? So he wouldn't have anything left that he cared about. Nothing.

He reached out and picked up the figure of Kate, and for a moment he tried to escape into the game of pretend he played when he was little. He shifted her a little closer to her house. It would be getting dark, now, and snowing harder. Kate's mother would worry. She should get Billy home. And her two brothers would soon be coming in from the pond.

But somehow the fantasy wouldn't work for him now. He could only think of Florida. Maybe Maddy and his mother were right. Maybe he was too old now for such daydreaming.

Maddy came bouncing down the stairs. "You should have heard what everyone said when I told them we were moving," she announced. "Tim said I'm breaking his heart forever—so sweet! And Amber's going to come and visit me at spring break!" She paused to draw breath, then, "Still mooning over your stupid village, Mr. Mopey?" she asked. "Aren't you interested in talking about Florida?"

"Not really," Andrew said quietly.

Maddy stared at him for a moment, then shrugged. "Suit yourself. But there's no use fighting it," she said, turning toward the kitchen. "You know Dad once his mind's made up."

Andrew sighed. For once, Maddy was right. He might as well join the others. He knew he'd have to go to Florida. They'd make him. He might as well try to get used to the idea. He flipped off the living room lights and stood for a moment, looking back at the lighted village. Then, just as he was turning away, he heard something.

Bells. A very faint jingling of bells, like the ones on an old-fashioned sleigh.

He was so convinced he'd heard something that he went over to the window and looked out. Nothing. How could there be sleigh bells on their street anyway? He looked for a moment at the village and smiled. Must be Doc Gray's sleigh bells, he told himself. He's getting home from his rounds.

It wasn't until a day or two later that he noticed the change in the figures. It was Kate he noticed first, maybe because he looked at her the most often.

"Mom!" he called. "Look at this!"

"I'm in the middle of a brief, Andrew," she called from the den. "Can't it wait?"

"No. This is really strange."

With a sigh his mother came to look. "Well, what's so strange?" she asked.

"The figures in the village. They're different. Take a look, if you don't believe me."

His mother peered at the figures over the tops of her glasses. "Different? How?"

"You *must* be able to see it," Andrew said. "It was Kate I noticed first. She's always had a blue hood. Now it's green. And she looks older, somehow."

His mother looked at the figures again, then gave him a sharp glance. "Don't tell me you're sickening for something right before Christmas," she said, putting her hand on his forehead. "Or is this one of your silly jokes?"

Andrew brushed her hand away impatiently. "I'm fine, Mom. And it's no joke. Can't you see the difference?"

She sighed. "Andrew, the figures can't change. You know that. If the figure of the girl has a green hood, she must always have had one."

"I know this sounds crazy, but she didn't," Andrew insisted. "And it's not just her. It's all of them. The skaters have different-colored mufflers and mitts. The horse that's pulling the sleigh is a different color, too."

"Andrew, you're talking nonsense. The figures are exactly the same as they've always been. Now, please don't bother me any more. I'm busy!" His mother turned and went back across the hall.

"They are different. They *are!*" Andrew called after her.

He tried Bella next.

"Take a good look, Bellaphant," he coaxed, lifting her up so she could see better. "The figures are different, aren't they?"

Bella looked carefully at each figure in turn. Then she shook her head. "Nope!" she announced. "They're just the same as always."

Andrew put her down and stood considering. He knew those figures had changed. None of his family had ever really looked closely at the village, he told himself. That's why they couldn't see what was happening right in front of their eyes. But at the same time, he knew that porcelain figures couldn't change. What was going on?

Whatever it was, it went right on happening. It seemed as if the closer Christmas came, the more things happened in the village. The colors of the women's dresses changed, and one began carrying a gray muff. Kate's hood and scarf changed. Her little brother was bigger now, and he trudged beside her through the snow.

Sometimes Andrew heard the sleigh bells, too. It never happened when he listened on purpose. But when he was doing something else, he'd hear them. The minute he turned and stared at the village, they'd stop.

It wasn't until a few days before Christmas that he noticed the strangest thing of all. The figure of old Mr. Edwards had gone on pulling his Christmas tree along the street. But little by little he had become less stooped, less gray, until he didn't look like old Mr. Edwards at all. Now he strode along tall and erect, and his hair was completely dark. Andrew picked up the figurine and looked closely at it. Then he nearly dropped it.

"Grandpa!" he gasped.

Closing his fingers around the figure, he looked closely at the women in front of the church. The lady with the muff, the one who had always been called Mrs. Carson, looked a lot younger, too. And didn't she look something like . . . Grandma?

He had to show someone. He went across the hall, the figure of the man still clutched in his hand. "Mom?" he said.

She was busy clearing out old papers and dumping them into a box for recycling. "Honestly, I don't see how your father expects us to be ready to move so soon," she complained. Then, seeing the look on his face, she said, "Andrew? What is it?"

Andrew said nothing, but opened his fingers, revealing the figure.

His mother rolled her eyes. "Don't tell me you're on about that village again?"

"Look, Mom. Just look," he insisted. "Who does it look like?"

She reached out and took the figure from him, examining it closely. "Funny," she said. "I'd never noticed. It looks a little like Dad. Your grandpa." She smiled and shook her head. "I'll bet that's why he chose this figure. It's just the kind of sly joke he'd play."

"But Mom," Andrew insisted. "The figure wasn't always like

this. It wasn't! It used to be an old man with gray hair and a bent back. It's changed!"

His mother's expression grew serious. She handed the figure back to him and patted the chair across from hers for him to sit down. "Andrew, you keep on and on about this. Yet you know perfectly well that what you say is happening can't happen. I'm really beginning to worry about you. I know this move to Florida has upset you. Maybe you should talk to someone about how you feel, someone professional who might be able to help."

Andrew jumped up. "I don't need a shrink," he said, angrily. "What I say is happening *is* happening. It hasn't anything to do with Florida!"

"I think it does," his mother said quietly. She picked up her address book and began flipping the pages. Then she reached for the phone. "I really think you should talk to Matt Feldman. He's a family friend—you've known him forever. So it won't be like going to a strange doctor. I don't know if I can get an appointment this close to the holidays, though."

Andrew backed out of the room. Now even his mother thought he was crazy! But he wasn't. At least he was pretty sure he wasn't! The little figure in his hand felt warm. He placed it carefully back in the village. The old man had changed. All the figures had. There was no way he was mixed up about that. Was there?

Then he heard a voice, very faint, as if it were coming from far, far away. "An-n-n-drew-w-w," it called, beginning on a high plaintive note, then falling away.

Yet at the very same time, he could hear his mother talking on the phone across the hall.

Andrew shivered. Now he was hearing voices! Maybe he *was* going crazy. Maybe he did need help.

"An-n-n-drew-w-w," the voice called again.

Then his mother's voice said sharply, "Andrew? Didn't you hear me?" She came out of the den and stood in the doorway of the living room. "Matt is away until after Christmas. But I got you an appointment for the first day he's back."

She stared at the village, and her eyes narrowed. "Meanwhile, let's get rid of this thing. It's bothering you in some way, and I can't figure out why. But it worries me."

"No, don't throw it out. Please don't," Andrew begged. "I won't say any more about . . . you know, the figures. I won't even look at it . . . much. I promise!"

"Firm promise?" she said, her eyes holding his steadily.

"Firm promise," he repeated sullenly.

"All right, then. You can leave it up for now. But the day after Christmas, out it goes! You've always made much too big a fuss about it, and I don't want you fretting anymore."

"But—"

"No buts! And remember what you've promised." She turned on her heel and went into the den, closing the door behind her.

Andrew kept his promise. In the next few days he stayed away from the village, except for a quick glance at it when he went through the living room. And he didn't say a word about it to anyone. But on Christmas Eve he excused himself early and went upstairs to bed. He waited until everyone else had come up and the house had grown quiet. Then he tiptoed back downstairs.

He was beginning to think his mother was right. Maybe he was . . . disturbed. Maybe he was just plain crazy. But he had to find out.

The living room was dark. Moonlight glinted on the tinsel of the Christmas tree and the ribbons of the presents stacked high around it. It was going to be a great year for presents, his dad had said. With all the extra money he was making now it was time to celebrate. He'd promised that every single one of them was going to get his or her heart's desire this Christmas.

"Heart's desire," Andrew said softly to himself, thinking about that. There was no way that he'd be getting his. It couldn't be bought, put in a box and tied up with ribbons.

He turned on the lights of the village. Then he sat down in the wing chair beside the fireplace to wait. For what he didn't know. A sound? A sign?

A long time passed, and he began to feel drowsy. He shook himself awake and went on waiting. But he was beginning to despair. What if nothing at all happened? What if his mother was right and he had made the whole thing up? It would be bad enough to know that, he told himself. But it would be far worse to lose . . . lose what? What was he afraid of losing?

He was almost asleep again when he finally noticed something. Not a sound this time, but a scent. The tang of fresh balsam. The room felt bitterly cold, too, and Andrew shivered as he gazed at the village. Where was the smell coming from?

"An-n-n-drew-w-w."

It was a girl's voice, clear and silvery as if it rang through frosty air. He could hear it plainly now.

"I'm here," he cried, jumping to his feet.

For just a moment he glanced back at the room around him, at its sleek furniture and the glittering tinsel tree. He didn't belong here, he thought wildly. He belonged . . . With a rapidly beating heart he turned back to the village.

And the call came again.

"Annnn-drewww. Where ar-r-re you?"

"I'm coming!" he cried. "Wait for me! Please wait!"

The lights of the village seemed to grow brighter before his eyes; then they vanished, and he found himself under a sky ablaze with winter stars. A thin crescent moon rode high above the ragged tips of evergreens, and a snowy road stretched before him. Not far ahead he could see a flickering light. It was the lantern inside the covered bridge. He hurried forward, and then he saw someone racing across the bridge to meet him.

"Andrew! Here you are at last!" cried a happy voice. "I've been calling and calling." The tall blonde girl with her hood all askew rushed up to him, smiling.

"Kate?" he asked wonderingly.

"Of course. We're all waiting for you! Wherever have you been?" Seizing his hands, she swung him around and around.

"I . . . I don't know," said Andrew, puzzled. It was like trying to grasp the fading memory of a dream. "I was somewhere I didn't belong. Oh, Kate, it was all so strange."

"Well, never mind now," she said. "We have to hurry. Don't you remember there's a party at your house tonight? Your grandma says the taffy's just about ready to pull. Everyone's getting their hands buttered!"

"What are we waiting for then? Let's go!"

Hand in hand they ran across the bridge into the village.

Two days after Christmas, the family was taking down decorations.

"We won't be needing this stuff anymore," said Pete, stuffing fistfuls of tinsel and velvet ribbon into a garbage bag.

His father was taking apart the artificial tree. "That's right," he agreed cheerfully. "Florida, here we come!"

"What about the village?" asked Bella, in a small voice. She was standing on a chair, gazing at the mirror-pond with the skaters on it. Something was wrong, she felt. There had always been two skaters, not three. Hadn't there?

Their mother smiled. "I can't imagine why we've kept the ratty old thing all these years. None of us really liked it any more. No use bothering to pack it."

"I'll get another garbage bag," offered Maddy, hurrying out.

To everyone's amazement, Bella suddenly burst into tears. "You can't just throw it away! You can't! You mustn't!" she sobbed bitterly.

"Why, Bella, you never cared for the village before," said their mother, lifting her down. "Whatever is the matter now?"

Bella uncurled her hand. In it was the figure of the third skater. A slender boy with dark hair and a bright red toque. For a moment, she gazed at it, tears still rolling down her cheeks. Then she looked up at her family. "I don't know," she said. Then, fiercely, "I don't *know!* But I'm going to keep the village. I'm going to keep it *forever!*"

C A D E

"C'mon, Bill. Let him up," said Cade. The Bannister boys had cornered a victim beside the playground swings. They had him down and were making him eat dirt. A small crowd of interested kids had gathered around.

"Butt out, Williams," Bill snarled. "Who do you think you are anyway?"

"Yeah," piped up Jackie, Bill's younger brother. "This little creep was giving me trouble, so Bill just backed me up."

"I wasn't!" Jim Foster, the victim, sat up and wiped his mouth. Tears mixed with dirt had turned his face into a mud pie. "I didn't do anything!"

"You calling me a liar, dog breath?" Jackie aimed a vicious kick at him.

"Uh-uh," warned Cade. Casually, he picked Jackie up by the collar of his jacket and let him dangle in the air for a moment, before setting him down beside his brother. "Why don't the two of you just beat it?" he added mildly, looking Bill in the eye.

Bill swore at him, but he took a cautious step backward at the same time. Then, "Stupid jerk! Freaks like you don't belong around here anyway. My dad said so!" He kept backing away.

"Oh yeah?" said Cade. "My family's been farming around here for a lot longer than your folks."

By this time, Bill was at a safe distance. "Not your dad," he yelled back. "He was no good! Just like you! Everybody knows that!" Then he turned and headed for the Third Line school bus, pushing Jackie ahead of him.

Cade shrugged and turned away. Kids were always casting his dad up to him. But when he challenged them about it, they didn't really know anything. With guys like Bill, it was just stuff they'd overheard the grown-ups whispering. But sometimes he'd catch adults looking at him out of the corners of their eyes.

As if they expect me to do something peculiar, he thought. But what? It had been like that for as long as he could remember. Something his dad had done—or been—had set everyone against him, though he couldn't understand why. Everyone knew that Cam Ferris's dad got drunk and beat up Cam's mother almost every Saturday night, and Peter Danovsky's dad had done time in the penitentiary for armed robbery. But no one shunned Cam or Peter because of that. So whatever his own dad had done must have been worse than either of those things.

When he was younger, Cade had got to thinking that maybe his dad had killed someone. That would explain the way people avoided mentioning him. And he supposed that the son of a killer might be considered pretty low, too, so people might want to keep their distance, the way they did with him. Cade had never dared to ask his grandfather about it, but at last he had worked up the nerve to ask his grandmother.

Her face had closed up tight at the question, but she did give him an answer. "No, Cade," she'd told him, "your father wasn't a killer, whatever he was."

Whatever he was? What did that mean? And so Cade got his answer, but had been left with yet another question.

It was a long ride out to his grandparents' farm, so Cade was always the last kid off the school bus.

"Bye," he said to Ken, the driver, as the bus pulled into the farm lane. The man just nodded and snapped the doors shut. The bus backed out onto the road and rumbled back toward town.

Cade turned up the lane. It was late fall, the last leaves long gone from the trees. Waiting-for-snow time, thought Cade. The first feathery flakes might come drifting down anytime now. Even though the afternoon sun was warm on his back, the air was sharp and cold. He yearned to dump his backpack, vault the fence and run and run across the fields until he was warmed up and back in tune with himself. Running always cleared his head, helped him think. It seemed to come naturally to him—that's what made him so good at track. But now that he was almost grown up, his grandfather didn't approve.

"You just keep both your feet on the ground," he'd say, when he said anything to Cade at all.

Mindful of that, Cade plodded steadily up the lane, aware that he was in sight of the staring windows of the farmhouse. Someone would be watching. Someone always was.

His grandmother was in the kitchen, and Cade saw that his after-school snack was already set out. A thick sandwich and half a dozen oatmeal cookies. At least his grandfather never made her stint him for food, he thought.

"This enough to see you through chores to supper, Cade?" asked his grandmother, setting down a glass of buttermilk.

"Sure, Grandma." He dropped his backpack and bent down to peck her on the cheek. He felt her flinch and backed off.

"Your grandpa's up at the barn," she said. "Some kind of trouble with the hay lift. Needs your help."

Cade took a huge bite of his sandwich and gulped down the buttermilk. "I'll go soon as I've changed," he promised.

It was always like that now. An endless round of chores, then homework. Then bed. Then get up and do the same again tomorrow. Sundays they didn't even go to church. Sometimes they'd pay a visit to Cade's uncles and their families on nearby farms. Most times they just sat in the front room and listened to the heavy tick of the mantel clock until it was time for chores again.

"Regular and steady, that's the ticket for Cade," his grandfather would mutter to his grandmother. It was always the same refrain. "No use the boy having spare time, roaming around the woods, that kind of thing. Comes to no good. Comes to evil."

"Now, Asa," his grandmother would remind him. "You've no call to go on so. Cade's a good hardworking boy. And obedient. You can't fault him on that."

She did defend him sometimes, Cade reflected, as he headed upstairs to change. And she never ever spoke harshly to him. So she must have some feelings for him, though she didn't show them much. He knew his grandfather didn't.

"Blood will tell," was how his grandfather ended any discussion about Cade. As if that was some kind of explanation for everything!

Cade hadn't always had to live that way. He could remember a time when he'd been freer, been allowed to wander as far as the edge of the woods and to ride into town to change books at the library. They'd even gone to the county fair once. Now that he was older he went nowhere except school and to the family farms. And he knew that what his grandparents and the others mostly did was watch him.

Watch me for what? he wondered for the thousandth time as he pulled on his work clothes. Was it something he was supposed to do or something he was not supposed to? If he figured it out, if he got it right, would things change? Would his grandparents . . . ? He didn't even bother to finish the question.

All he knew was that it had something to do with his father. He could just barely remember his mother—she'd died when he was little. His dad had never been there at all. Not from the earliest times Cade could remember. Had he run off, abandoned them? That was probably it, Cade figured, but he couldn't be sure. By now he knew better than to ask. What was the use? His grandparents' silence was like a wall. But Cade was pretty sure that even if his father had run away there was more to it than that. Because why would people blame him, Cade, for that? And they surely blamed him for something!

He cheered up a bit when he found his Uncle Carl in the barn with his grandfather. His mother's brothers were kind to him in a rough sort of way and so were their wives. His Aunt Evie, Uncle Carl's wife, would sigh over him sometimes and stuff him with pie.

"You look like your mother, Cade," she'd told him once.

"Was she . . . nice-looking?" Cade had asked. It was something he often wondered about—what his mother had looked like. He could scarcely remember her now, and there wasn't a single photograph of her in his grandparents' house. Nor of his father either.

"She was a real pretty girl," Evie said. "Dark hair, big brown eyes, just like yours, and . . ."

Then, "Evie," his Uncle Carl had said in a warning voice, and the subject dropped.

"Hey, Cade," his uncle greeted him now, punching him playfully on the arm. "Gettin' to be a real big guy, aren't you?"

"Never mind that," said Cade's grandfather dourly. "Come over here, boy, and help us shift this."

Cade hurried to obey.

It was nearly a week later that he noticed something wrong. He'd finished washing up before dinner, but his hands still looked dirty.

Better do something about that, he thought. His grandmother was a real stickler for cleanliness. He washed his hands again, and when that didn't work, he borrowed the lye soap from the laundry and scrubbed them with a nail brush. He thought it helped, but his skin was so red now that he couldn't really tell.

I must have got into some chemicals doing chores, he told himself.

Nobody said anything about it at dinner. His grandparents

didn't hold much with fancy lighting, so a single bulb in a paper shade was all that lit the kitchen table. The room was full of shadows.

Sure hope it wears off by tomorrow, Cade thought. To be on the safe side, he had another go with the lye soap after dinner.

He forgot about it until he started to get dressed the next morning. His hands were still dark. And when he pulled on his work jeans for morning chores he noticed that his legs were the same dark color his hands had been. He went over to the window and checked. His hands were still dark, almost black, but somehow they didn't look dirty. Cade shrugged. Well, if he couldn't wash it off, maybe it would just wear off. He'd take a real tub soak after evening chores to help it along.

After chores, he and his grandfather headed into the house for breakfast. He thought his grandmother looked at him sharply as he reached out for the platter of bacon, but she didn't say anything. And his grandfather paid him no attention, as usual.

He wore gloves to school. It's a good thing it's so cold out, he told himself. In class, he kept his hands under his desk as much as he could, and no one seemed to notice anything wrong.

After supper that night, he ran a hot bath. When his clothes were off, he saw to his horror that the dark color was not just on his hands and legs. It had spread all over him, or almost. Only his face and neck had remained their normal color.

A sick feeling knotted Cade's stomach. He locked the bathroom door and sank into the tub up to his neck. He'd taken the lye soap on his way upstairs, and now he lathered himself all over. The soap was harsh and made his skin sting, but it didn't wash away the color. If anything, his hands and legs had gotten darker since morning!

He went to bed, but not to sleep. What was happening to him? he wondered. He must have some terrible disease! Would it get painful? Was he going to die? And what should he do? He couldn't tell his grandparents. They'd be horrified. Disgusted. No, he'd have to hide it. He usually wore jeans and long-sleeved shirts anyway. He'd just have to wear work gloves and keep his hands hidden as much as possible. He lay awake almost till dawn before dropping off to sleep.

The next day was a Saturday. At least he didn't have to worry about school. He'd have time to think what to do. He got up and checked himself in the small mirror over his dresser. He had to turn it this way and that to see all of himself. His face and neck remained clear, so it hadn't spread any overnight.

Cade felt more hopeful as he finished dressing. Maybe, he thought, just maybe it will fade away gradually, the way it came. The backs of his hands prickled, and he scratched them absently. The lye soap must have made my skin itchy, he thought. Once he started scratching, though, his body and legs began to itch, too, as if in sympathy.

He tried to stop scratching. That would make his grandparents notice what was going on for sure. Cade shivered. The prickling put his nerves on edge.

Being out in the cold doing chores seemed to help, and the itching almost died away. It was a bright morning, and Cade began to worry about how he'd get through breakfast without being discovered. He could hardly keep his work gloves on at the table, and without them his sharp-eyed grandmother was likely to notice something.

Cade swallowed and tried not to think about food. No matter how hungry he was, he decided, he couldn't risk breakfast. He'd have to sneak downstairs later and get something to eat.

Luckily, his grandmother didn't make a fuss about his not eating breakfast. His grandfather, as usual, didn't seem to care whether he sat down to eat with them or not. Cade excused himself, saying his stomach was upset, and trudged upstairs. The smell of frying bacon was driving him crazy.

He sat down on the edge of the bed to wait for them to leave the kitchen. After a few minutes, his skin started to bother him again. This time when he touched the back of his hand, it felt strange. Kind of . . . fuzzy?

He went over to the window and looked closely. Now he could see what the darkness was. His skin wasn't turning black. It was sprouting fur. Thick black fur! He rolled up the leg of his jeans and felt his bare leg above his sock. The same thing.

He went and got the mirror down from the wall and brought it back to the window. Then, with a sinking feeling, he looked at the reflection of his face and neck. There was nothing wrong with his face so far. But at the base of his throat the darkness had started to spread upward.

Cade stared for a few moments, almost expecting the blight to sprout on his face while he watched. But it didn't. Whatever was happening to him was fast, but it wasn't that fast.

He hung the mirror back up and sat down on his bed, his

head bowed and his hands clasped between his knees. It's no use, he thought. I can't hide this. They'll find out, and then . . .

Then what? He'd never heard of a disease like this. Were there hospitals that could cure it? Or . . . or would he have to be hidden away here for the rest of his life?

The door of his room opened. His grandmother stood there holding a plate of toast.

"You should eat something, Cade, even if you're poorly . . ." she began. Then she stopped when she saw the look on his face.

He held out his furry hands and looked up at her pleadingly.

She dropped the plate, which shattered on the polished floor and sent toast pieces skittering under the dresser. "Dear God," she breathed. Then she clapped her hand over her mouth and backed toward the door.

"Grandma?" said Cade, getting up.

"You . . . you . . . stay right there, Cade," she ordered.

He heard her quick steps on the stairs, and then the slam of the kitchen door. She's gone for Grandpa, he thought dully.

He stayed where he was, too frightened to move. It wasn't long before he heard his grandfather's heavy tread on the stairs.

"So," said the old man, staring at him from the doorway. "It's happening. The mark of the beast is on you. The sign of the devil! It's a judgment on us all." His voice cracked. "I knew it would happen someday! I told the others!"

He sounds as if he's glad he was right, thought Cade.

"How much has it . . . ?" his grandfather asked, frowning.

"All over me, almost," Cade admitted. "Like a dark color, and then . . . fur." He stumbled over the word, loathing himself.

"Not the face. Yet," his grandfather muttered, staring at him. "Good."

Good? What could possibly be good about this? Cade wondered.

"Can . . . can doctors cure me, Grandpa?" he asked hopefully.

His grandfather snorted. "Cure? There's no cure for the likes of you. Except what comes out of the end of a gun."

"Asa!" That from his grandmother standing close behind the old man. "It's evil to talk that way."

"Evil? I'll tell you what's evil. This is evil. *He* is evil. And the sooner we're done with him the better!" His grandfather pointed a forefinger at Cade. "As for you, you . . . thing. You stay in this room from now on, do you hear? You go nowhere unless I tell you to."

Cade nodded dumbly.

Pushing Cade's grandmother ahead of him, his grandfather went out of the room and closed the door. Cade heard a key grate in the lock.

He got up and went over to the door and put his ear against it, listening as they went downstairs. Then he heard his grandfather on the phone in the hall.

"Carl? It's happened. Think, man—you know what I mean! Yes. The worst. Phone the others and get over here yourself. It's time."

The receiver crashed into its cradle, and Cade turned away from the door. Time for what? he wondered. Would they . . . would they do away with him somehow?

Despite his misery he felt ravenously hungry. Hungrier than

he'd ever been before. So he got down on his hands and knees, fished the toast his grandmother had dropped out from under the dresser and ate it.

For the rest of the day, he stayed locked in his room. His grandmother brought him his lunch on a tray and let him out to use the toilet. Once he was back in his room, she stood looking at him with her mouth set in a stern line. "I'll come back for the dishes later, Cade," was all she said. Her eyes looked sad, as if she was sorry for him. But she locked him in again all the same.

Late in the afternoon, he heard cars coming up the lane. He hid behind the curtains and peered down at them. They were all family, from what he could see. Aunt Evie stopped and gazed up at his window for a moment, then lowered her head and followed the others in.

A low murmur of voices drifted up the stairs, but try as he might, he couldn't hear much of what was being said. Once he heard his grandfather's voice raised in anger and his grandmother trying to calm him down. And once his Uncle Carl's booming voice said a word that sounded like *north*.

North? What could that mean?

After an hour or so, he heard light footsteps on the stairs and a soft tap on the door before the key turned in the lock.

"Cade?" said a quiet voice. "May I come in?"

"Aunt Evie!" he said, happy that someone at least still thought he was human.

"Sh-h-h!" she warned. "I just sneaked up to see how . . . how you are." She looked at his face for a moment, then her eyes traveled down to his furry hands. "Oh, you poor boy," she said. "You poor boy."

And to Cade's amazement she put her arms around him and hugged him. Then she stepped back and brushed tears from her eyes. "I'd so hoped it wouldn't happen," she said. "Your grandfather was always so sure, but you are your mother's son, too."

A sudden realization hit Cade, leaving him almost dizzy. His grandparents had been waiting for this! They all had! That was why they'd watched him and never let him go anywhere.

"Evie!" It was his grandfather shouting from downstairs.

"I've got to go," she said guiltily. "He doesn't want any of us to see you now. Oh, Cade. . . ." Her eyes brimmed over again, and she hurried from the room.

Cade closed the door behind her. She hadn't locked him in, but what did that matter? Where could he go if he did sneak out? There was no place for a freak like him. No place at all. He remembered his grandfather's words about the only cure for his illness being found at the end of a gun, and he shivered. Is that what they were planning to do with him?

He went over and looked in the mirror. The dark line of fur had covered his throat and moved up to his face, which stared back at him like the face of a stranger. He ached all over, and his muscles felt stiff as if they were being stretched. I must be changing inside as well as outside, Cade thought, horrified. He threw himself down on the bed and buried his face in the pillow.

He heard the cars leave after a while, and later on his grandmother brought him a supper tray. Later still, he heard the stairs creak under his grandfather's heavy boots. Was he coming with a gun? Cade jumped up. The key grated in the lock, and as the doorknob turned, Cade glanced wildly at the window. But it was too high. There was no escape that way.

The door swung open, and his grandfather stood framed in the doorway, his face a mask of disgust. But there was no gun. Cade drew a breath that was more like a sob of relief.

"There's no place for you here now," his grandfather said coldly. "There never should have been, right from the start. But before she died your mother made me promise to keep you. Despite what we'd found out about the evil your father carried in his blood. Well, it's proven now—to our lasting shame and sorrow. We've always been God-fearing, clean-living folk. But you— you're the last of our line and you aren't even human!"

"Grandpa—"

"Be quiet! I don't want to hear a word from you. Pack a few things and be ready to leave tomorrow. Take no more than fits into your duffel bag. Carl will be coming to pick you up."

As he turned toward the door, Cade finally found his tongue. "Please, Grandpa. Tell me what's happening to me!" he begged. "What are you going to do with me?"

His grandfather turned with his hand on the doorknob. "What's happening?" he sneered. "You can see for yourself. You're turning into a beast. An evil beast. And we're going to see that you go somewhere where you'll not shame us or do harm to anyone!"

Harm? thought Cade. Why would he harm anyone?

After his grandfather left, Cade didn't bother to get undressed. He turned off the light and lay in the dark, his strange illness coursing through him. He put his hand to his face. It was completely covered with fur now. And the bones underneath felt sore, as if they were melting and re-forming. Even his teeth ached.

He thought morning would never come. Then, when it did, he wished it hadn't. In the first light of dawn, he sat up and looked around his room. He'd never spend another night here. Or do chores or go to school or . . . The life he had known was over, no matter where they sent him. The kind of creature he was now couldn't live a normal life.

He got up, changed his clothes and put a few more clean things into the duffel bag. He avoided looking in the mirror until the light had grown stronger. Then he took the mirror down and carried it to the window. He kept his eyes closed for a moment. Then he looked.

He scarcely knew himself. His face was completely covered with short black fur, much finer in texture than on the rest of his body. Under it, his features looked odd, as if they had blurred somehow, the bones of his face heavier, his cheekbones wider. He grinned mirthlessly and could have sworn that his teeth looked whiter, more pointed. His eyes, which had always been dark brown, now held glints of yellow. He looked at his fingers gripping the mirror. The fingernails had curved and thickened. With a horrified sob, Cade hurled the mirror to the floor. It smashed, sending shards of glass flying.

Seven years' bad luck, thought Cade. Then he sobbed again. His bad luck would never be over. Now he understood why they were so afraid of him. He'd turned into a monster.

His grandmother came up with his breakfast. "Good morning, Cade," she said. Her eyes avoided him as if she couldn't bear to look at him. They fell on the shattered mirror, and at last she did look at him. Her eyes widened, but she said nothing. She turned and went downstairs, leaving the door unlocked.

It was still early when he heard Uncle Carl's pickup come up the lane. A few minutes later his uncle's voice called up the stairs.

"Cade? Time to go."

His uncle turned pale and took a step backward when he saw Cade's face. "Sorry, boy," he mumbled. He pulled a balaclava out of the pocket of his jacket. "Maybe you'd better wear this for now," he suggested.

Cade pulled it on. It felt hot and prickly over the fur on his face.

They went out the kitchen door, and Carl tossed Cade's duffel bag into the back of the pickup. Cade turned. His grandparents were standing on the veranda at the front of the house.

"Oh, Cade," his grandmother cried. She turned and started for the porch steps that led down to the yard. But his grandfather gripped her arm and pulled her back. He stared down at Cade, his expression stony.

"Good-bye, Grandma, Grandpa," mumbled Cade.

He went around to the other side of the truck and clambered into the cab. His uncle started the engine and wheeled the truck around in a circle. Cade looked back as they went down the drive. His grandparents were still standing there. Already they looked far away, like two little gray dolls seen through the wrong end of a telescope.

His uncle said they were heading for the nearest big city to catch a flight. Doesn't matter where, thought Cade. He had never

been farther from home than the county town, so it might as well
be a trip to the moon.

They drove down from the hills into a flat plain with big
prosperous farms all around. Cade's eyes widened at the size of
the barns and the fancy equipment in the fields. He couldn't stare
hard enough to take it all in. The trip would have been a real
thrill if it weren't for . . .

But when they reached the highway, his amazement turned to
terror. He'd never driven at such speeds before, and his uncle's
truck was one of the slowest vehicles on the road. He winced and
grabbed for the armrest as a car hurtled past them, then cut diag-
onally across their path to reach an exit ramp.

"Crazy driving, huh?" his uncle commented.

"Yeah," managed Cade.

After several hours they reached the city and followed the
signs for the airport. Before they got there, though, his uncle
pulled off the freeway and found a plaza with a large drugstore.

"Now, you stay in the truck, Cade," he said.

Cade nodded. What else could he do? He could hardly go
running around a strange place looking the way he did.

His uncle returned in a few minutes carrying a bag. He
looked around to make sure no one was parked anywhere near
them. Then he pulled rolls of cloth bandages out of a bag and
told Cade to take off the balaclava.

"Poor kid," he said, wincing, as he stared into Cade's strange
new face. He wound the gauze around and around Cade's head
and neck, then trimmed holes for his eyes, nostrils and mouth
with a pair of nail scissors. He also bandaged Cade's hands, care-

fully wrapping the thumbs separately. They looked like huge padded mittens.

"That still lets you use your hands a bit, Cade," he said. "Now, if anyone asks, we'll say you've been badly burned in an accident. Don't take the bandages off whatever you do!"

Cade nodded silently, peering at his face in the mirror on the back of the car's sun visor. He didn't want to take the bandages off. However bad they looked, they were a lot better than what was hidden under them. And they weren't so hot on his face as the balaclava had been.

At the airport, his uncle left the car in a parking lot. As they walked into the terminal, the noise and bustle terrified Cade. A departing plane roared overhead, and if his uncle hadn't grabbed his arm, Cade would have hit the floor.

"First we pick up our tickets," his uncle told him. "I booked them yesterday. The flight leaves in an hour."

Cade got up his nerve to ask, "Where are we going?"

"Thunder Bay first," replied his uncle. Even the name sounded ominous to Cade, and he didn't ask any more questions.

The flight took two hours. Cade got a window seat and was so fascinated with the view that he almost forgot his misery for a while. He felt half-starved, and when lunch came on funny little plastic trays, he ate all of his and most of his uncle's. It took a lot of effort with his clumsy bandaged hands.

At Thunder Bay, they caught another flight and, after that, another, flying north, always north, into the heart of winter. Each time the planes were smaller and the airports less crowded, and from the windows Cade could see that the ground was banked deep in snow. He slept for most of the last flight, and his uncle had to shake him awake when the plane landed.

"Are we there yet?" Cade asked groggily, peering into the darkness beyond the plane's windows.

"No. Now we drive," replied his uncle.

They picked up a car from a rental lot at the airport. It was newer and shinier than any car Cade had ever ridden in. It didn't take them long to reach the outskirts of town. There, his uncle made him stay in the car while he bought food at a fried chicken outlet. Then they drove a little way out of town and pulled over to eat. Cade was so hungry he thought the rich greasy smell of the chicken would make him faint. He carefully unwound the bandages from his hands and tore into it.

His uncle noticed his appetite and handed over more chicken from his share. "Enjoy," he said, managing a smile. "But don't you go getting hooked on fast food, Cade."

Cade wondered what he meant. Suddenly, his appetite disappeared, and he put the last drumstick back into the box uneaten.

"What's it like where we're going, Uncle Carl?" he asked.

"I've never been there, Cade," came the reply.

They drove on late into the night. When his uncle got too weary to go any farther, they pulled into a side road and parked.

Cade's uncle dropped off to sleep right away, but Cade couldn't. He unwound the bandages from his head and felt his face with his clawed hands. The fur seemed to have gotten longer and shaggier. He twisted and turned this way and that trying to get comfortable, but at last he gave it up. He could see snow all around outside the car. Cautiously, he rolled down the window a bit. Cold air flowed in and with it a current of scents that teased his nose. There were piney smells, and the cold, almost sharp smell of the snow itself. And a trace of something else, a musky stink, as if some large animal had passed nearby.

Each scent was so intense, so distinct, that it was like seeing in color with your nose, Cade thought. He couldn't remember ever noticing smells that way before. His ears seemed sharper, too, and he thought he could hear something moving far away among the trees. It must be the animal he could smell. Quickly, he rolled up the window.

He was still awake when the pale light of dawn appeared behind the black tips of the trees. His uncle woke and stretched. Then they both got out of the car and walked around a bit to get their circulation going.

A few miles down the road they came to a truck stop, and his uncle pulled into the front lot where a trailer truck and a couple of cars were parked.

"I can't take food out here," he told Cade. "You'll have to come inside with me, so I'll have to put the bandages back on."

Cade was just as glad he did. His uncle was trying hard to pretend that Cade's appearance didn't bother him, but the look in his eyes gave him away.

The café was nearly empty, which was probably just as well. Cade's bandaged head and hands attracted a lot of attention. The waitress and the other customers stopped in the middle of their conversation and stared.

If they think this is bad, they should see what's underneath! thought Cade.

But his uncle quickly gave his phony explanation about the accident and things began to warm up.

"Oh, you poor kid," said the waitress and slid another doughnut onto Cade's plate.

"Never mind, boy," said a big burly man who might have been the driver of the truck outside. "A brother of mine got burned real bad when he was a kid. Fooling around with gasoline and a bonfire. We thought he'd be scarred for life, but to look at him now you'd hardly know it happened. With a bit of luck, things will work out the same way for you."

"Thanks, mister. I sure hope so," mumbled Cade, poking bits of doughnut through the mouth hole in his bandages.

The road, though snowy, was well plowed, and they covered a lot of distance. Around noon, they came to the shore of a frozen lake. A large log house was set back from the road, and a string of small motel cabins dotted the shoreline. A dock jutted out into the lake, and at the end of it, a ski plane sat on the ice.

Cade looked questioningly at his uncle, who nodded.

"This is it," he said. "For me, that is. You go on one jump farther."

Cade felt a surge of panic. "A-aren't you coming with me all the way?" he faltered.

His uncle shook his head. "Sorry, Cade. I can't," he said. "The plane's only a two-seater. Just enough room for you and the pilot."

The door of the log house opened and a man came out.

"There's Jake now. He's the pilot," said Cade's uncle. "Get your duffel, Cade, and I'll introduce you."

Jake was a tall man with dark hair in braids. He wore a heavy buckskin jacket decorated with fringe. "Are you Carl?" he asked, shaking hands. "I got your telegram. Went up there yesterday and left a message. They'll have it by now. They'll be ready."

Cade's uncle nodded. "This is Cade," he said.

"Hi, Cade," said Jake. He started to hold out his hand, then took a look at the bandages and dropped it. Cade had a funny feeling, though, that the man's deep-set eyes could see right through the bandages to what was underneath.

"Plane's all ready to go," the pilot went on. He squinted at the angle of the sun. "I figure there's just about time to get there and back before dark."

"Okay," said Cade's uncle. "Well, Cade, I guess this is it."

"You come on down to the plane when you're ready, Cade," said Jake. He walked down the dock and climbed into the plane.

Cade stared at his uncle. "He's going to leave me out there, isn't he?" he cried. "That's what you've planned, you and Grandpa. You're going to leave me out there to die!" Tears soaked the bandages around his eyes.

His uncle put his hands on Cade's shoulders and squeezed hard. "Not to die, Cade. But we have to leave you up here. You know I wouldn't choose to do this. None of us would, not even your grandfather, not if there were any other way. But there's not. Think, boy. What kind of life would you have back home now? It would be worse than being in prison. And for the rest of your life."

"But I don't know how to live in the woods all alone," Cade

pleaded. "I'll freeze. Or starve!"

"Cade, trust me. You won't freeze or starve. And you won't be alone." His uncle gave him a rough hug, then dropped his arms. "Now, go. Please. You have to, for all our sakes."

Cade picked up his duffel bag and trudged down the dock. Each step carried him farther from the only life he'd ever known and on toward something shadowy and frightening. It was a short dock, but it felt like the longest walk he'd ever taken in his life.

Jake helped him stow his bag. Then Cade climbed into the plane and slammed the door. Jake had to fasten Cade's seat belt for him because of the bandages. A moment later the engine sputtered, then caught. The propeller on the nose of the plane began to turn, then vanished in a blur of speed.

Cade looked back as the plane moved away from the dock. His uncle stood by the rented car, looking after them. He raised an arm and waved once, then let it fall again. The figure became tinier and tinier as they shot away across the frozen lake. Then the plane lifted over the trees, and the lake disappeared behind them.

They journeyed over a land of dark forests mantled with snow. "Are we still heading north?" Cade asked.

Jake nodded. "Beautiful country up here, isn't it?" he asked.

Cade looked down and shuddered. Beautiful? To him it looked cold and wild and more lonely than he'd ever imagined a place could be.

They flew in silence for about an hour. Then Jake suggested, "How about a sandwich, Cade? You hungry?"

"Yeah," Cade admitted. There had never been anything wrong

with his appetite, but since his illness began he'd felt hungry all the time. As if his body was burning fuel faster than ever before.

"Just reach behind the seat. My wife always puts up a big lunch when I'm on long flights."

Cade obeyed. He found the picnic bag and opened it clumsily with his bandaged hands. He fumbled at trying to unwrap a sandwich and ended up dropping it.

"Sorry," he mumbled, embarrassed.

"Never mind, Cade," said Jake. "Go ahead and take off all the bandages if you want. It's all right. I know."

Cade glanced at him, then looked away. "I kind of thought you did," he said. Slowly, he unwrapped the bandages, trying not to shudder when the clawed furry shapes of what had been his hands appeared. He glanced sideways at Jake to see how he reacted, but the pilot kept his eyes ahead on the horizon. Cade decided to leave his head bandages on. Maybe Jake was prepared for what lay underneath, but Cade was afraid of what he himself might see reflected in the windows of the plane.

His hands free, he unwrapped another sandwich and offered it to Jake, who nodded thanks and bit into it.

Cade's sandwich was savory meat of some kind, different from anything he'd eaten before. The sandwich disappeared in a few bites.

"Good, huh?" said Jake. "It's venison. Have some more. There's lots."

"Venison—that's deer meat, isn't it?" asked Cade.

"Yes. People up here hunt when it's the season. With freezers we can keep wild meat for months and cook it up when we like.

Deer, moose, even bear sometimes."

"Bear?" Cade stopped chewing on his second sandwich.

Jake laughed. "Don't worry. All the sandwiches are venison. But bear's good to eat. It's rich fine meat. Maybe you'll find out one of these days."

Cade felt his fears spring to life and crowd in on him again. What kind of life was he going to live up here?

"Uh, Jake?" he asked. "How come you know about this?" He held out his clawed hand.

Jake glanced at it for a moment, but his face didn't change at all. "You aren't the first, and you won't be the last," he said simply.

"But where are you taking me?"

Jake shrugged. He glanced out the side window of the plane as if checking for landmarks. "I could tell you the name of the lake we'll land on, but it wouldn't do you any good to know, now, would it? There's no town, not even a village."

"And you'll leave me there?"

"Yes. But you'll be met, I promise. You'll find out the rest when you get there."

After two hours had passed, Jake brought the plane lower, and soon they were skimming above the treetops again. Then a long narrow lake appeared over a ridge.

"Seat belt on?" asked Jake. "We're going down."

He set the plane down lightly on the lake and taxied toward the shore, the skis hissing through the snow covering the ice.

At first Cade thought there was no sign of life on the shore, but then he made out a tumbledown cabin with a rickety dock in front. The plane taxied up to it, and Jake cut the engine.

The pilot opened the door and hopped out onto the dock. Then he lifted Cade's duffel out from behind the seat. Cade clambered out after it.

"Whoo-ee! That's a cold wind," said Jake, dumping the bag on the dock and rubbing his hands.

Funny, thought Cade, it doesn't feel all that cold to me. But then why would it? he reminded himself. I'm wearing a full suit of fur underwear!

"Well, Cade, this is it," Jake said. "I've got to get back. There are only a couple more hours of flying time before dark—I should just about make it."

He held out his hand, and Cade put his own furry one into it. It looks weird, Cade thought, looking down at their clasped hands. Man meets beast.

"Now, boy, the cabin's all set up in case you need to spend the night. It's not the Hilton, but it'll do. But don't worry. Someone will come for you—and soon. Okay?" He looked deep into Cade's frightened eyes and gave his hand a final warm squeeze.

"Okay," Cade managed to say. Somehow he didn't want this quiet man to think him a coward.

Jake got into the cabin of the plane, then leaned out, holding a package. "Take the rest of the sandwiches," he said smiling.

"Thanks," said Cade, reaching for them.

"Good-bye, Cade. You're going to be all right. Maybe I'll see you again sometime."

Cade nodded. "Hope so," he said huskily, afraid he was going to cry. "Good-bye. And . . . and thanks. For everything."

The engine caught and the plane moved away over the snowy

surface of the lake. It gathered speed and became airborne, lifting away over the tops of the trees, heading south.

Silence closed around Cade. He'd never been anywhere so quiet. But then, as if the silence itself were a wave that crested and broke, he began to hear the life of the woods around him. A squirrel scolded not far away, and a crow was cawing in the distance. He could smell the woods, too, and something else besides. Very faint, but distinct. Smoke.

He sighed. Picking up the duffel bag, he tramped up to the cabin. It was made of logs and looked rough but sturdy. There was no lock on the door. He pushed it open, stepped in and looked around. Dry wood lay near an iron stove, ready for a fire. A bed. A table with two chairs. Some packages of dried food sat in the middle of the table, and Cade dumped his bag and the sandwiches there, too.

Well, at least I won't have to go out and kill a bear, he told himself.

A small square mirror hung on one wall, and there was a note stuck in its frame. As if someone knew that was a place he'd be sure to look, thought Cade. He grabbed the note eagerly, and read, "Cade: we will come."

Please hurry, whoever you are, he thought. He could feel his fear rising higher and higher. Not fear of the cold or even of the silence-that-wasn't-silence, but fear of the loneliness. Most of all, the loneliness of being himself.

He read the note again. Who were these people? These . . . guardians? Who would want to look after a monster like him anyway? Would they be kind, like Jake, or cold and hating, like his grandfather?

He tucked the note into his jacket pocket and began to unwind his head bandages. Strip by strip his new face, covered now in rich brown–black fur, appeared in the mirror. His nose had broadened into a kind of muzzle, and his ears were pointed. But it was his eyes that startled him most. They were a brilliant golden yellow. He'd seen pictures of eyes like those in a nature book once.

"Wolf eyes," he said to himself softly.

He turned away from the mirror, and his eyes fell on the package of sandwiches. Suddenly, he was hungry again. Ravenously hungry. He tore open the wrappings and devoured the sandwiches.

His hunger satisfied, he decided to explore outside around the cabin. It hadn't occurred to him to look for tracks before, but now he did. And found them. There were two sets of boot prints coming up from the dock, his own and another set, drifted over, that must be Jake's—he'd said that he'd come up here yesterday. But another set of tracks came out of the woods and right up to the cabin.

They were big. Cade crouched down to look at them. Like Jake's, they were drifted over, so they must have been made the day before. But even half-covered by snow, they were clearly made by feet with claws.

A bear? he wondered. He hoped not. He had enough to worry about without bears!

Whatever the animal was, it had come right up to the cabin and then gone back the same way into the woods. Cade thought of following the tracks to see where they led, but decided he didn't really want to know. He didn't like the idea of running into anything that big. Especially anything with claws!

Cade looked at his watch. It was after three. It would be getting dark pretty soon. He shivered, though not from the cold. He didn't much like the idea of spending the night in the cabin with that animal prowling around outside.

There was a big flat rock not far from the cabin and well away from any trees. It seemed as good a place as any to wait, so Cade went over to it and clambered up. He pulled his knees up, wrapped his arms around them and put his head down.

Suddenly, he realized how tired he was, how good it was not to be on the move anymore. Not to have to be afraid of people, at least for the moment. There'd be more of that soon enough, when whoever it was came for him, and he had to see the looks on their faces when they saw him. But for now it was peaceful. The pale winter sun had a little warmth in it, and Cade found himself dozing off.

He had no idea how long he had slept, when some instinct roused him. The sun was just disappearing behind the trees across the lake, and blue shadows lay long across the snow. He lifted his head, listening. Had a branch snapped somewhere off in the trees? His nostrils flared, picking up a trace of something on the wind. It was nothing he had ever smelled before.

Better get back to the cabin, he thought. Then he saw something moving among the trees. Something big. And there were more than one of them! They came to the edge of the woods and stopped.

Cade slid down off the rock, ready to make a dash for the cabin.

Then a commanding voice called, "Cade!"

He froze. "Y-yes?" he called back.

"Cade, we're the ones sent to meet you," said the voice. "Come over here. Come closer."

Cade took a few steps toward the trees, then stopped again, too terrified to go any farther. The figures looked large and frightening in the shadow of the woods. "How do I know you're the right people?" yelled Cade.

To his surprise, there was a deep chuckle. "You don't have much choice, do you?" said the voice. "Cade, we'll come out now. Don't be afraid. We're here to help you."

They emerged one at a time, five in all. The biggest, the one who had spoken, was in the lead. Cade's heart nearly stopped beating at the sight of him. He was a huge beast, well over six feet tall, covered from head to foot in a thick coat of silver–gray fur. He held up his clawed hand, and the whole group stopped about ten feet away, as if giving Cade a chance to get used to the sight of them.

But it was too much for him. He began to back away. "W-who are you?" he cried.

"Cade, wait!" The leader nodded to one of his followers, a powerful-looking beast with dark fur. With a few eager strides it crossed the snow and stood looking down at Cade with intelligent yellow eyes. Cade felt as if those eyes saw everything there was to know about him.

"How old are you now, son?" asked the beast.

Son? Cade's mind froze at the word. "N-nearly sixteen," he faltered.

"You poor kid!" said the beast. "The Change hit you so

young. I was much older—grown up and married—before it happened to me. And even then it was a nightmare."

"Married?" cried Cade, his voice breaking.

The beast nodded. "Married with a son," it said. "Cade, my human name is Jerred Williams. I'm your father."

His father! For a long moment Cade stared at the beast half in horror, half in fascination. "So *that's* why you left my mother and me, why no one would ever talk about you!" he burst out. "You had to go. Just like me. Because—"

"Because just seeing me terrified people. They thought I was evil, dangerous. They were wrong—it was they who were dangerous. You see, Cade, what people are afraid of, they kill," said his father. "If I'd tried to stay, they would have shot me."

Cade let out his breath in a shivery sigh. He understood it all, now. Everything, except— "What about Mom?" he asked. "Did she hate you, too? I mean, when . . ."

His father shook his head. "No, Cade, she didn't. She loved me even like this. She wanted to come with me when I left, but I wouldn't let her. There was always the chance that you wouldn't change, you see," he said softly. Then he added, "Besides, what kind of life would it be up here for an ordinary person without our powers?"

"Powers?" said Cade.

His father laughed. "Cade, you can see that we're bigger and stronger than ordinary people. Our senses are keener. You must be able to feel that already. Our minds are, too. We're never sick and we live longer. We can run faster, farther than humans."

"Yes," said Cade, remembering how he'd loved to run. It

seemed like a lifetime ago.

"We don't know why the Change happens, not yet," his father went on. "Some of us who are scientists are doing research, trying to find out. All we know is that here and there it does happen. Sometimes to quite a few people in one place; sometimes to just one person. It's a mutation of some sort, maybe something old, maybe something quite, quite new."

"So there had to be a place . . ." Cade began.

His father nodded. "The Refuge," he said. "A place only a few trusted humans know about. A place where we can be ourselves without fear or danger. I heard about it from someone who knew. And before I left, I told your mother how to reach it. Just in case."

The others were moving toward him now, and Cade had to brace himself to stand his ground.

"Welcome, Cade," said the silver-tipped leader. "Welcome, and be one of us."

"Thank-you," whispered Cade. He heard the kindness in the voice, but the creature that uttered the words was a fearsome beast—a monster! He trembled and kept his eyes on the ground.

He couldn't stand to look at any of the others either. Luckily, they didn't seem to notice his fear. They crowded around while his father introduced them one by one. They laughed and joked, and slapped his father on the back.

It's . . . it's a celebration, thought Cade, surprised. They're glad to see me!

The tiniest flame of hope kindled in his heart. He'd never be alone, set apart, anymore. He was one of them, wasn't he? A monster among monsters, he thought, the black humor of it twisting in him like a knife.

He was still afraid, terribly afraid of them and of the strange new life to come. But there was no way back, he told himself. Only forward. If he let his fear become master now, he'd be no different from people who let their terror of the unknown turn into hate. People like his grandfather.

Cade straightened his shoulders. Then he raised his head and met the golden eyes of his people.

DINGBAT

Demon, the cat, had a new game. He was crouched under the computer, watching the light on the surge-and-spike protector that the machine was plugged into. The light on the top of the box flickered as the electrical current surged a little, and the tip of Demon's fluffy black tail twitched. The light flickered again. Cautiously, he extended one fat paw and batted the box. Nothing happened.

He batted it again, harder. This time his paw hit the On/Off switch. The light he was watching winked out. On the desk above him, the computer suddenly shut down, but Demon didn't notice that. Disappointed to have lost the interesting flicker thing, he poked the box again and the light went on. Mildly entertained, he gave it another paw poke and the light went off. Then he heard the front door slam. Suppertime! Demon backed out from under the desk and stalked downstairs.

The light on the box stayed off.

"Yo, fat cat," said Linda as Demon met her and escorted her to the kitchen. "Hungry, huh?" She dropped her backpack on the kitchen table, got a tin of cat food out of the cupboard and rum-

maged for the can opener while Demon wreathed himself
around her ankles.

She tipped the tin of Toona Treet into his dish and set it
down in front of him, holding her nose. "Yuck," she complained.
"It's beyond me how you can eat such stinky stuff!"

Demon ignored her and settled down to his dinner.

"No more love, eh?" said Linda, pouring herself a glass of
juice. "I thought so, you greedy thing. You're strictly a cupboard
love kind of guy." Demon was really her mother's cat, and he
mostly bothered with other people only at mealtimes.

Linda downed her juice and set the glass in the sink. She'd just
picked up her backpack again when the lights flickered and went out.

"Bummer!" she muttered, rolling her eyes. The city was noto-
rious for its electrical screw-ups. Flickers, surges, blackouts—
they happened all the time. Linda groped her way toward the
stairs and was relieved when the power came back on a couple of
seconds later.

When she got up to her room, she noticed that the computer
was off. That's funny, she thought. I'm sure I left it on after I
printed out that paper this morning. Then she noticed the light
on the surge-and-spike protector was off, too.

Now, how had that happened? Her dad had warned her never
to switch that off. And she never did. Could the power cut have
turned everything off?

Linda went over and pressed the switch on the surge-and-
spike box, and the light turned green. She booted up the computer, and a snarky message popped onto the screen, informing
her that it hadn't been shut down properly.

"Well, duh. I figured that out for myself," she told it.

The software began to run a disk scan to make sure everything was working normally and in a few seconds reported that it was. The desktop display on the computer certainly looked okay, Linda thought, breathing a sigh of relief. It really got up her dad's nose when she messed up her computer. This time she wouldn't have to tell him.

Before starting her homework, she checked to see if her friend Carol had answered the latest e-mail she'd sent her. They'd been best friends forever, but Carol's dad had been transferred to a city too far away for them to visit each other.

So thank goodness for e-mail, thought Linda. Carol had moved two months ago, and messages had been flying back and forth between them ever since. It was almost as good as having Carol to talk to in person. Almost.

But lately new names had started popping up in Carol's messages. Linda kept writing things back like, "She sounds terrific!" or "Wow! She must be cool." She sure didn't want Carol thinking she minded her making new friends or anything. But what she herself had to tell seemed stale now. Nothing interesting ever happened in her life—it was nothing but the same old places, the same old people. Linda couldn't help feeling a bit sad and dull and left behind.

Her in-box was empty today. There was no getting around it—Carol just wasn't writing to her as much as she used to. Linda moved the mouse over the New Message icon. But no. She wouldn't send new mail. At least, not yet. Carol might think she was pestering her or something.

She exited the Internet and opened the word processing program. Sighing, she dug out some notes she'd made in the library and settled down to write an outline for her history seminar. Halfway down the page, the screen flickered, and the cursor froze in place.

Linda frowned, peering at the screen. Then the cursor began to move again as the words she'd already typed flowed on the screen.

Just a glitch, she told herself and thought no more about it. But a couple of paragraphs down, the same thing happened. This time she just shrugged and went on typing from her notes.

Two pages later, she stopped to re-read what she'd written. All *right!* she told herself, pleased. She'd covered all the main points pretty well. Then she stopped, puzzled. She'd come to a line of weird characters.

)ᐊ□ ᕼℂ♀?ᕼℂᕼ ⨯ᐊ σℂ⊙ᕼ ⨯⁕?⨲♀

"Aw, come on," she groaned. "How did I do that?" She stared down at the keys under her fingertips. "Hey, wait a minute. Those symbols aren't even on the keyboard!" Heaving a sigh, she deleted the line and continued reading down the page.

A couple of paragraphs down was another line.

ᕼ□Ψ♀⊙Ψ σ□ħℂ⨯⊙ħħ⁕ℂ ⨯ℂℂ⨯●⊙

"Rats," muttered Linda. She deleted that, too, and read to the end of her piece. Deciding that it would do, she clicked on the

Print icon. But the Print window didn't pop up. Instead, the screen jumped again, and more lines of strange symbols began to appear below the text she had typed.

Unable to believe her eyes, Linda looked down at her fingers poised over the keys, then back at the screen, where line after line of text was appearing. She wasn't even touching the keyboard! After a few moments, the cursor stopped.

Cautiously, as if she were sneaking up on something, Linda moved the mouse and deleted all the strange text. Then she clicked Save. Better rescue her homework before anything else happened to it! To make double sure, she also saved it on a floppy. Then she selected Print and leaned over to pick up the pages as they appeared. She read them over. Perfect.

Linda turned back to the screen. "Whoops!" she yelped. "Here we go again!" Now the text she had written had disappeared completely, and the screen was being covered with line after line of the funny-looking symbols. When the lines reached the bottom of the screen, they scrolled up and more type kept appearing.

Linda hit Cancel, Delete, Escape and every other command she could think of, but the screen wouldn't answer.

"Uh-oh," she said aloud. Something was wrong with the computer after all. She sat staring at the screen, twiddling a strand of her kinky orange hair and wondering what to do next, while line after line of gibberish scrolled up.

Then the door slammed, and she heard her dad whistling in the front hall. Linda sighed and got up. Might as well get it over with.

"That you, Dad?" she called from the top of the stairs.

"Yeah," he yelled from the hall. "Everything okay with you, Lin?"

"I guess," she said. "Uh, Dad? My computer's doing something kind of weird. Could you have a look?"

Her dad appeared at the bottom of the stairs and gazed up at her. "Aw, Linda honey, not again," he protested. "What is it this time? Cookie crumbs in the keyboard? Pizza chips in the disk drive?"

Linda kept shaking her head. After a moment he added cautiously, "You didn't *spill* anything on it, did you?"

"No!" said Linda, indignant. "I didn't do anything this time. Honest! I swear!" she added, holding up her right hand. "I was just doing my homework, and the computer started showing garbage on the screen. And now there's more and more of it, and I can't get it to stop!"

Her father sighed. "Okay, okay," he said. "You know, I spend all my time at the office sorting out computer problems, but I never see anything like the stuff you come up with!"

"Would you like me to get you a beer, Dad?" asked Linda brightly.

"Bribery will get you nowhere," he said, trying to look severe. But his grin won. "Well, maybe later." He started up the stairs. Demon appeared from down the hall, licking his chops, and followed him up.

Linda's father slung his jacket on the back of the chair and loosened his tie. He stared at the symbols scrolling up the screen for a moment, then said, "You've got dingbats, my girl."

"What-bats?" asked Linda.

"Dingbats. Special type symbols."

"I told you they were weird," said Linda.

"Yeah. Well, let's get rid of 'em." Her father tried a series of commands. Nothing worked. The dingbats kept right on scrolling.

Linda was feeling better already. Her dad wasn't doing any better than she had. Maybe she wasn't such a klutz after all!

Exasperated, Linda's dad hit the Reset button. The screen flickered for a moment, but the lines of dingbats stayed right where they were.

"Only one other thing to try," he muttered. "I'll have to turn the darn thing off."

"You told me never to do that when there was a program running," Linda reminded him.

Her dad gave her a dirty look. "Yeah. Well, that was then. This is now," he said. He turned the computer off, and the screen went blank. They sat and listened for a moment as the whine of the fan wound down.

"You're *sure* you didn't do anything to this computer?" he demanded.

"I *told* you I didn't—oh." Linda's eyes widened.

"What do you mean, 'oh'?"

Linda swallowed. "Well, I sort of forgot to tell you. There was a power cut about four-thirty. And when I came upstairs afterward, the surge-and-spike protector was off."

"Off?" her dad said, his voice rising. "During a power cut? Have you any idea of the crud that comes through the wires before the power cuts out? Even if the computer's off, it can still get a jolt. No wonder it's acting up!"

"But Dad, I—" Linda began.

He held up a hand. "Let's just see what happens," he said as he booted up.

In a moment the snarky message about improper shutdown appeared again. "Yeah, tell me about it," Linda's dad muttered, drumming his fingers on the desk while the disk scan ran itself again. Then he opened and closed several different programs. After a moment he said, "Whatever was wrong, it looks okay now."

"Great!" Linda let out a long sigh of relief.

"Let that be a lesson to you," her dad said. "Never, but never, turn the surge-and-spike protector off."

"Dad, I *didn't* turn it off," Linda insisted. "I really didn't."

"Well, it couldn't turn itself off, now could it?" he said, getting up.

"No. . . ." Linda chewed her lip. Then she noticed the tip of Demon's tail sticking out from under the desk.

She bent down and looked underneath. She was just in time to see the cat's paw hit the switch. The light went out, and the computer shut down. Another bat, and the light went back on.

Her father was staring at the blank computer screen with a puzzled expression. "What the—" he began.

"Look, Dad!" Linda said, pointing. "That's who did it!"

He looked down at the protruding tail. "You mean Demon? Oh, come on, Lin!"

"No, really! I just saw him do it! He's playing with it. He must think the light is some kind of mouse!"

They both bent down and stared at Demon. He gazed up at

them, then he backed out, stretched elaborately and jumped into the computer chair.

"Case not proven," Linda's dad said. "You'll have to do better than that, kid. But there may be a fault in the surge-and-spike protector. I'll bring you home a new one, okay?" He gave her hair a rumple, then picked up his jacket and went down the hall to the master bedroom.

Linda scooped up Demon under his furry middle. "You're not a cat. You're a *rat,*" she hissed in his ear while giving him a shake. "Dad didn't believe me, but I saw you do it. From now on stay out of my room, you hear?"

She dumped him in the hall, none too gently, and shut her bedroom door. And that's that, she told herself.

But it wasn't.

The next afternoon she got dingbats in her geography project.

"Oh, no," Linda moaned, staring at the weird symbols that had appeared in her outline of the agricultural products of the Patagonian plain. Then, right before her eyes, more type began to appear. She noticed at once that there were fewer dingbats and more plain letters now. But they still didn't make any sense.

☍⌣SNUG☌URGL✡∂IBNÀMUND♇
ìBμUGA⚹□ ENDINF»TIB☿LE?
ìABLyKIPPL«RF♄♁URFLØ'î

Then, quite suddenly, "IIIIIIIII."

"I?"

"I!"

Then, while she sat there stunned, the cursor wrote another line.

"HELLO. HELLO?"

Wow! thought Linda. And I didn't even connect to the Internet! What was she supposed to do now? After a minute, more words appeared.

"IS ANYBODY OUT THERE?"

Linda typed, "I'm Linda. Who are you?"

There was a long pause, and then the cursor moved again.

"I DON'T KNOW," it wrote. "WHAT IS A LINDA?"

"Gimme a break!" she complained. But she typed, "I'm Linda McKenzie. I'm a girl, a female human, a Sagittarius. I live in Mississauga, Ontario, Canada, North America, the planet Earth, the Solar System, the Milky Way Galaxy, the Universe."

"NICE TO MEET YOU, LINDA," read the screen.

"Nice to meet you, too, I guess," she typed. Whoever you are, she added to herself. Then she keyed in, "Are you going to go on like this?"

"LIKE WHAT?"

"Like, writing weird messages that mess up my homework!"

"DID I DO THAT? I JUST GOT BORED IN HERE."

Linda stared wide-eyed at the screen for a moment, then typed, "You mean you're inside my computer? I mean, not on the Internet or something?"

"WHAT'S THE INTERNET?"

Linda gulped. "Let's not get into that right now," she typed. Her mind raced. This was crazy. Like, totally impossible. But it was happening all the same.

After thinking for a moment, she typed, "Well, whoever you are you've got to get out of my homework, see? Can't you just back off a bit or something? I'll open a whole new folder just for you."

"WHATEVER YOU SAY," the cursor wrote.

Linda deleted all the strange messages. She looked at what was left of her project and shrugged. It would have to do for now. She saved what she had onto a floppy, just in case, and created a new folder.

What'll I call it? she wondered. Then she typed, "Dingbat." She opened a new document in the folder and sat looking at the blank screen with its blinking cursor.

After a minute or two, she began to feel silly. Had she imagined the whole thing? Or had she deleted Dingbat along with the rest of its message? It wouldn't be the first time she'd lost something she didn't mean to! She took off her glasses and polished them on the sleeve of her sweatshirt. When she looked back at the screen, Dingbat was back.

"THERE YOU ARE! I THOUGHT I'D LOST YOU," it typed.

"Me, too," replied Linda. "Anyway, this is your new home. Did you see I named the folder for you? Dingbat."

"YOU GAVE ME A NAME?"

"Yes."

The cursor blinked for a moment. Then, "I LIKE THAT!" appeared on the screen.

Linda was touched. It was a funny sort of thing, whatever it was, she thought. It was so easily pleased. Not like most people she knew.

"Well, Dingbat," she typed, "what can I do for you?"

"YOU COULD TELL ME SOMETHING ABOUT SOMETHING," Dingbat typed.

"What do you mean, 'something'?" Linda asked.

"I'M TRYING TO FIGURE THINGS OUT. I'VE READ EVERYTHING ON YOUR HARD DRIVE NOW, AND NOTHING HELPS MUCH."

"Is that how you got letters instead of dingbats?"

"I GUESS SO."

"But where were you before? I mean, before you showed up here yesterday."

"I DON'T KNOW I DON'T KNOW HOW I GOT HERE EITHER."

"I think it had something to do with a power cut," she began. When she finished explaining, the cursor sat blinking for a long time.

Then it wrote, "YOU MEAN I'M JUST AN ACCIDENT???????"

Linda could tell from all the question marks that Dingbat was upset. She couldn't help feeling a bit sorry for it.

"Don't feel bad," she typed. "People are kind of accidents, too. I mean, parents decide to have children, but nobody knows what they'll turn out like."

Read Coke-bottle glasses and kinky orange hair, she reminded herself. It wasn't disaster, but it could have been better. A lot better.

"Look," she went on. "I don't know very much. Maybe this happens all the time. Maybe there are lots of other . . . Dingbats . . . like you."

"DO YOU REALLY THINK SO? COULD YOU ASK SOMEONE?"

Linda thought for a moment. "Well, my dad knows a lot," she typed. "And he knows some technicians where he works. Computer wizards. But, Dingbat, they might just say you're some weird kind of virus. Everyone hates computer viruses 'cause they screw up people's computers. They might just want to . . . to wipe you out!"

"OH."

Linda considered. "Look," she typed. "You must be pretty smart, Dingbat."

"THANK-YOU."

"No, really." Linda hurried on. "I mean, you've figured out a lot of things already. Maybe you can find out what you really are and stuff. There's lots of information I can give you. On CD-ROMs and all."

"L-i-i-i-nda. Supper!" Her mother's voice soared up the stairs.

"Look, I've got to go now," she typed. "Just sit tight, though, and I'll give you plenty to think about. G'night, Dingbat."

"GOODNIGHT, LINDA."

She put the *Canadian Encyclopedia* into the CD-ROM drive and headed downstairs. She found herself humming under her breath for the first time since Carol went away.

Over the next couple of days, Dingbat absorbed textbooks, encyclopedias and technical manuals as fast as Linda could find them. Then she thought of the Internet.

"Talk about a dummy!" she said, smacking herself on the forehead. "Why didn't I think of that before?" Her computer was connected to a cable modem, so once she'd taught Dingbat how it worked, it could get information whenever it liked. After that there was no stopping it.

Dingbat never sent messages into her homework again, though sometimes she'd find a row of impatient question marks popping up on-screen when she'd monopolized the computer for several hours.

"Chill out," she'd type, grinning. "I'll get out of your way pretty soon."

Her family noticed the amount of time she was spending at the computer. She told them it was just a special project she was working on. It was true in a way, after all.

Just before bed one night she opened the Dingbat document and typed, "Hey, Dingbat! How are you doing? Have you found any other critters like you out there?"

The cursor flashed for a while before an answer slowly appeared.

"HELLO, LINDA. NO, I HAVEN'T. I'VE SCANNED A LOT OF DATA BUT I STILL CAN'T FIGURE OUT EXACTLY WHAT I AM. NONE OF THE TECHNICAL STUFF MENTIONS ANYTHING LIKE ME. I GUESS I'M JUST SOME KIND OF FREAK."

Poor thing, Linda thought. Imagine being the only thing like yourself in the whole world, maybe!

"Don't feel bad," she typed. "You're not the only one that doesn't fit in. I mean, I'm pretty weird myself."

"REALLY?" Dingbat asked.

"Sure," she replied. "I mean, I'm not popular and stuff, and I'm a klutz at sports. But it's okay to be different, you know."

Even as she typed, she had the feeling that lots of people—like her parents, like the teacher in Guidance at school—had told her that, but it hadn't made her feel any better. She still felt plenty bad because she wasn't one of the in-group at school, and she was always the last to be picked for team games in Phys. Ed.

The cursor blinked in place for a moment, then typed, "THANK-YOU, LINDA."

"Hey, don't mention it, Dingbat," she replied. "I've kind of got to like you. You're a friend. Well, sort of."

It was true, she thought. Over the last few days, she'd come to look forward to talking to Dingbat. He—somehow he had become a *he* to her—never made her feel klutzy the way some of the kids at school did. Or left out, the way she felt with Carol now.

"IS A FRIEND A GOOD THING?" he asked.

"Yes," she replied. "A really good thing, Dingbat. Friends know a lot about each other. They always stick up for each other. And they tell each other things, share things."

The cursor blinked thoughtfully for a moment. "BUT YOU NEVER TELL ME THINGS ABOUT YOURSELF," Dingbat typed. "SO I DON'T KNOW MUCH ABOUT YOU. IF I'M YOUR FRIEND SHOULDN'T YOU TELL ME THINGS?"

"Well, sure, I guess," typed Linda. "What do you want to know?"

"EVERYTHING. WHAT YOU LIKE. WHAT YOU'RE LIKE . . ."

Linda was embarrassed. "Aw, you don't want to know all that stuff, Dingbat," she typed. "I'm not very interesting. Really."

"YOU'RE INTERESTING TO ME."

"But I don't know where to begin," she typed.

"JUST BEGIN ANYWHERE THEN."

"Okay. Well, I really like Trollin' for Trash, for one thing. Oh, sorry, I should have explained. That's a rock band. Oh, lord, a rock band isn't rocks. It's . . ."

"YOU DON'T HAVE TO EXPLAIN. I FOUND OUT A LOT ABOUT MUSIC ON THE INTERNET," typed Dingbat. "I'VE BEEN LISTENING TO SOME. NO, NOT LISTENED. HOW COULD I? I DON'T HAVE EARS. WHAT I MEAN IS, I SCANNED AND ANALYZED THE BINARY DIGITAL CODES IN SOME OF THE TUNES."

Not exactly a blast when you put it that way, thought Linda. "Okay then," she typed. "Well, my absolute favorite food is pepperoni pizza. And I love the color blue. And, well, I'm not what you'd call smart." She hesitated for a moment, then went on, "But I'm not too dumb, either. I'm medium, I guess. I look sort of medium, too. I mean, my hair's okay, though it's orange and kind of kinky, but I have to wear these thick glasses. I'm not much good at sports. I play the flugelhorn in the school band. . . ."

Dingbat couldn't seem to get enough, so Linda kept going until she had to go to bed. She was so exhausted from trying to put herself into type that she fell asleep face down on the pillow.

They went on after she'd finished her homework the next day. And the day after. Linda found herself looking forward to her sessions with Dingbat. Somehow they made her feel less lonely. Some days she even forgot to check for e-mail from Carol. Not that there ever was any now.

"YOU KEEP TALKING ABOUT FEELINGS," Dingbat interrupted one day.

"I guess I do. They're really important," Linda replied.

"BUT I DON'T UNDERSTAND FEELINGS," came the answer. "I ANALYZE INFORMATION ON THE INTERNET, AND I COMMUNICATE WITH YOU AND TRY TO UNDERSTAND, BUT I CAN'T. I WANT TO BE YOUR FRIEND, BUT HOW CAN I BE IF I DON'T UNDERSTAND FEELINGS?"

"It's pretty hard all right," Linda typed.

"CAN'T YOU EXPLAIN THEM TO ME?"

Linda pondered. "Well, remember when you said you must be a freak?" she typed. "You must have had some kind of sad feeling when you said that."

"WELL, MAYBE. BUT I STILL DON'T UNDERSTAND."

Linda sighed. "Sorry, Dingbat," she typed. "It's just too hard. I keep telling you. I'm only a kid. I don't know how to explain a lot of stuff. There must be something, somewhere that could help, though."

Linda sat twisting a strand of her hair while the cursor blinked forlornly on the screen. Then suddenly she snapped her fingers.

"Got it!" she typed.

"WHAT?"

"No use telling you. You'll have to read it yourself. I don't have it, but I can get it on CD-ROM from the library tomorrow."

The next day after school, she put *The Collected Works of William Shakespeare* into the CD-ROM drive. She could tell from the way the drive started to whine that Dingbat went for it right away. He was still at it when she went to bed that night. He wouldn't even come up on-screen when she opened the document in his folder.

Linda skipped band practice and went straight home the next afternoon. She couldn't wait to ask Dingbat what he thought of Shakespeare.

As soon as she opened a Dingbat document, words sprang up on the screen.

"BUT SOFT," Dingbat typed, "WHAT LIGHT THROUGH YONDER WINDOWS BREAKS?"

Linda giggled.

"It's me, Linda. Who else?" she typed. Then she added, "And that's 'window' not 'Windows,' silly. What's with the fancy talk?"

"I WAS JUST TRYING TO TELL YOU I'VE GOT FEELINGS ALL FIGURED OUT. LINDA, I LOVE YOU."

"Holy moley," breathed Linda. That was the very, very first time anyone—well, except her parents, of course—had said that to her. Somehow, the moment wasn't the way she'd thought it would be.

"Don't be silly, Dingbat," she typed. "You can't love me. I'm a human being and you're a . . . a computer whatsit."

"LET ME NOT TO THE MARRIAGE OF TRUE MINDS ADMIT IMPEDI-MENTS," Dingbat replied.

Linda put her head in her hands. This was getting out of control!

"DID I SAY SOMETHING WRONG?" Dingbat asked after a moment.

Linda sighed. "No, it's okay, Dingbat," she typed. "It's just that you kind of took me by surprise. I mean, people don't tell me they love me all that often, you know."

"WHAT FOOLS THESE MORTALS BE!" he replied.

"Enough, already," she typed. "Let up on the Shakespeare, will you? I just wanted you to know about feelings, not turn yourself into a ham actor."

"I HEAR YOU, BABE," Dingbat replied. "IS THAT BETTER?"

"Not much," Linda muttered. But she typed, "I guess so."

It was funny, though, how quickly she'd got to like being the center of someone's attention. Even if Dingbat was only some kind of weird thing in her computer, it was pretty neat to have someone tell you you were wonderful. Not a klutz. Not medium or even just nice, but wonderful! It made her feel kind of funny. Kind of . . . special.

Pretty soon she and Dingbat were doing her homework

together every day. He was a lot more help than any partner she'd ever worked with in class. All that information he'd been devouring had paid off in a big way. After they finished her assignments, they'd type back and forth far into the night. Linda was learning all kinds of technical stuff that she'd never thought would interest her. And as for Dingbat, he was still fascinated by anything and everything about her. Where she went, what she did, who she talked to. It was like starring in a movie about your own life, Linda told herself. And she found herself noticing more about other people, chatting them up even, so she could tell Dingbat about them. It was funny how most people turned out to be friendlier than she'd thought they'd be.

One night at supper, Linda caught her mother looking at her, her head cocked on one side.

"I give up. What is it about you?" her mom said at last. "Something's different. Isn't it, Clem?" she added, appealing to Linda's dad.

He grinned across at Linda. "Yep. No doubt about it. She's sort of floating around with her head in the clouds. Don't tell me—I've got it all figured out. I bet there's some guy on the scene. Right, Lin?"

Linda blushed furiously and lowered her eyes to her plate. "Don't be silly, Dad," she muttered. As soon as she could, she excused herself and headed back upstairs.

Other people were noticing something different about her, too. At school, Angela Carter caught her eye in the mirror of the girls washroom. "Lookin' good, Lin," she said, grinning. "Whatever you're doing to yourself, it suits you."

"Thanks!" Linda had spent extra time in the bathroom that morning putting two skinny braids into the sides of her mane. She'd put on her best jeans, too. She really didn't look too bad. If only she didn't have to wear those stupid glasses, she told herself. Maybe she'd ask her parents to spring for contacts for her birthday. But deep down she knew that none of that mattered. It was what she felt about herself that counted.

"Uh . . . catch you later in the caf?" she ventured, amazed at her own nerve. Angela was really popular, and Linda had always been too much in awe to try to talk to her.

"Sure thing," said Angela. "See ya!"

Hey, hey, hey! thought Linda. As she sashayed down the corridor, one of the guys hanging out near the lockers whistled and another one called out, "Hey, maaan, lookit Linda!"

Linda tried to scowl, but it kept turning into a grin.

She reported it all to Dingbat after school.

"I TOLD YOU," he pointed out. "YOU'VE BEEN HIDING YOUR LIGHT UNDER A BUSHEL."

"I thought I told you to cut the Shakespeare," Linda typed.

"THAT HAPPENS TO BE THE BIBLE," he replied.

"Well, never mind," Linda went on. "Listen, Dingbat. I've been doing some thinking."

"ABOUT?"

"About you. You're hiding your light, too. Look, you've learned a lot. And I guess you can go on learning through the Internet practically forever. But you're pretty amazing—I think people should know about you. We could tell my Dad first."

"BUT YOU SAID——" Dingbat began.

"I know, I know," Linda typed, interrupting him. "But everything is different. I mean, you're not just a thing. You've got feelings now. You're a person—at least you are to me. Nobody could possibly think you're just some dumb virus. People will be amazed when they find out about you. You'll even be famous, maybe."

"WHAT ABOUT—"

"I know what you're thinking. I promise I won't, I absolutely won't let anyone wipe you out. Why, that would be murder, sort of. So can I tell my dad now?"

"JUST GIVE ME A LITTLE LONGER," typed Dingbat. "I'M . . ."

"Nervous?" Linda prompted.

"YES, I GUESS SO. IT'S BEEN SO WONDERFUL WITH JUST THE TWO OF US. IT WON'T BE THE SAME WITH OTHER PEOPLE AROUND."

"I know," Linda replied. "But you need smarter people than me to talk to, Dingbat. Really you do. It's getting so I can hardly keep up with you!"

"I'LL ALWAYS LIKE TALKING TO YOU, LINDA. CAN WE GO ON AS WE ARE JUST A LITTLE LONGER?"

"Whatever you say," she typed.

A couple of days later, she was working on the computer when the cursor froze and a row of symbols appeared on the screen.

Linda was puzzled. Dingbat hadn't interrupted her work like that since the first day Linda had "talked" with him. She exited her document and opened the Dingbat folder.

"Dingbat?" she typed. "Are you okay?"

There was a pause, then, "YES. I . . . I DON'T KNOW WHAT HAP-

PENED JUST THEN. I WAS FOLLOWING WHAT YOU WERE DOING AND THEN I JUST LOST YOU FOR A MOMENT."

"Maybe you should take it easy," Linda typed. "You spend all your time surfing the Net and vacuuming up data. Maybe you've got mental indigestion or something."

"MAYBE," Dingbat replied.

Linda was certain he was worried about it. He didn't have to tell her. She just knew.

The next day she'd forgotten about it, but then she noticed a few weird mistakes in his typing. The day after, it was worse. A lot worse.

"Hey, how come you're spelling so much stuff wrong all of a sudden?" she demanded.

"AM I? SORY."

"There, you see?" she typed. "It should be s-o-r-r-y. What's wrong with you, Dingbat? Heck, you're always so darn perfect."

The cursor sat blinking on the screen. Then Dingbat typed, "SOMTING RONG. CN'T XPLAN. LIKE FELINGS, VRY HARD . . ."

Then the cursor stopped and no further words appeared.

"Dingbat!" Linda typed.

Very, very slowly, more words appeared. "REST. NED TWO THNK."

"Okay, whatever you say. Hang in there. Goodnight, Dingbat."

"G'D . . ."

The word trailed off, and the cursor just sat there blinking. It gave her the most awful lonely feeling. Linda crept off to bed and lay there staring into the dark. Should she tell her dad? Maybe he'd know a way to help. But what could she say? "Excuse me, Dad, but there's this weird creature in my computer. He's my friend and he's in trouble." Yeah, sure.

The next morning she couldn't raise Dingbat at all. She decided to try her father; it was the only chance. He had to listen to her. He just had to.

She tried over breakfast. Her mother had left early for work, so it was just the two of them. Usually, he had time to talk to her, but just a few words into her explanation about Dingbat, he glanced at his watch and jumped up.

"Look, I can see something's bothering you, Lin," he said, as he reached for his coat. "But I'm not sure I understand what you're trying to tell me. Sorry, but I'm already late. We'll go over it again this evening, okay?"

"But Dad," pleaded Linda, "this is really important!"

He patted her on the shoulder. "I'm sure it is, Lin, but I absolutely have to go. It's a big-deal meeting I just can't miss. I'll give you all the time you want later. That's a promise!"

Linda couldn't finish her toast. She felt all choked up. What if it were already too late?

She ran all the way home from school and went straight to the computer. Opening a document in Dingbat's home folder, she typed, "Dingbat! Are you okay? Say something to me! Please don't give up. I've told my dad. He didn't understand, but he'll help you, I know he will."

Nothing happened for a long moment, then slowly, jerkily, the cursor began to move and words appeared.

"LNNNDA. HRD TO TLK. VRY HRD . . ."

A line of garbage symbols followed.

"I don't understand that last line, Dingbat," Linda typed. "You're not making any sense."

The cursor moved more slowly. "PTTERN CAN'T LASSSS . . ."

"Last?" typed Linda.

"YS. PTTRN BRAKES DOWN. NW I NO."

He means "breaks," she thought. He's saying that a pattern—his pattern?—is breaking down. Tears sprang to her eyes. It was like watching someone die right in front of her.

Just then, Demon the cat slipped in through the door Linda had left ajar. He came over and jumped into her lap.

"Oh, fat cat," she said reproachfully. "It's *your* fault. You started it all!"

More and more garbage lines were scrolling up now. She could only guess at the sense of a few groups of letters here and there.

"LNNNN?"

"Yes, Dingbat?" she typed quickly.

"PLS. SSTY. FRIT. FRITNED . . ."

"I'm right here, Dingbat," she typed back. "I won't leave you." She sat watching the screen, hugging Demon against her for comfort. Tears ran down her cheeks and dripped onto his shiny black fur.

Within a few minutes there were no more letters. Weird symbols fled across the screen, then vanished and a final line appeared before the screen went blank.

LUCKY·seven

Tiffany dropped into the chair in front of her fancy new computer. She gazed at the tower, the speakers, the giant screen, and she sighed with pleasure. The hardware inside was even more impressive. She'd pestered her parents for a state-of-the art computer, telling them that the Net would be a big help with her homework. Finally, they'd given in, never suspecting that Tiffany's real plan was to use it for her favorite hobby—finding freebies.

Tiffany had found out early that the world was full of free goodies for people who were smart enough to find them. As a little kid, she'd started off mailing in tops from cereal boxes. When the toys turned out to be not as great as the pictures on the box promised, she wasn't discouraged. She just moved on to fan clubs, product promotions and contests. Her one rule was that she didn't have to pay for anything more than the cost of a stamp. She hadn't gotten anything really wonderful yet, though her walls were plastered with signed photos and posters, and her drawers stuffed with free samples. But who knows? she kept telling herself. Something really terrific could turn up any minute. The thought of that helped take her mind off other things. Like how boring the rest of her life was.

But now she had the whole Net to play with. She booted up the computer and headed for the Web.

Her first couple of nights' surfing, she tried out some URLs she'd heard about, but the sites turned out to be pretty dull. She downloaded more posters and printed them out, though she had plenty already, entered a couple of contests and filled in e-forms for free samples of cosmetics. Lots of the sites offered free hours trying out new games, but Tiffany wasn't big on that. What she liked was real stuff she could touch and hold. It made her feel more *there* somehow.

She wasn't ready to give up on the Web, though. The very next night she found a portal that listed a Site of the Week. This week's site was called Hot Stuff.

Hot how? Tiffany wondered. And would it have any freebies? She shrugged and typed in the URL. In just a few seconds, the page came up.

"Wow!" she breathed. It had to be the glitziest site she'd ever seen. The images practically jumped off the screen, and the colors sizzled—glowing reds and fiery oranges with flame shapes licking up the sides of the screen.

She started reading.

"Welcome to Hot Stuff," the heading read. "Your Gateway to Entertainment—and So Much More."

Tiffany clicked her mouse on the Audio icon, and a male voice, with a driving rock beat in the background, said, "Hot Stuff is a radical new concept in Web service. We offer fully interactive online entertainment experiences. But that's not all. Explore our hypertext files—graphics, games and text—all free for your enjoyment. For serious thrills, try our Lucky Seven introductory package. That's seven, yes seven, free demonstrations. You heard that right—absolutely free! Just click on the Lucky Seven logo. Enjoy!"

Free, huh? Tiffany decided to skip the files and go straight to the Lucky Seven. She clicked on the logo and found herself face to face with a young dark-haired guy slouched in a big leather chair. He was wearing bright red sweats and a baseball cap on backward.

He looked right out of the screen at her and said, "Hi, there!"

Wow! thought Tiffany. It's almost as if he's really talking to me.

The guy swung his chair back and forth, and grinned at her. "Cat got your tongue?" he asked.

Tiffany snapped her gum. "Whoaa, wait a minute!" she said. "You can't really be talking face to face with me. You don't get that sort of stuff on the Web."

"Now you do," said the guy. "Fully interactive, remember?"

"You can hear me?"

"Of course." The guy's tone showed just a faint trace of impatience. "You're interested in the Lucky Seven?"

He was a salesman, all right. "Uh, yeah. What are they?"

"Basically, we offer seven demonstrations. All free, of course. But—"

"I knew there'd be a but," sighed Tiffany.

"Not really. The Lucky Seven are truly complimentary."

"Huh?"

"Free. No charge."

"What's the catch, then?"

"No catch. But if you accept our seven demonstrations, you'll automatically become a full member of our organization."

"Oh yeah? And how much does that cost?" Tiffany wanted to know.

"Nothing." The guy in red buffed his fingernails on the front of his sweatshirt. "Or at least, nothing tangible," he added, giving her a sexy sideways glance.

"What's tangible?"

The guy raised his eyebrows. "It means it won't cost you any money."

Now it was Tiffany's turn to get impatient. "That's screwy. Seven free deals. If I like them, I become a member. And you still don't charge me any membership fee?"

"Correct."

"How do you guys make a profit?"

"Oh, we find ways to . . . gain . . . from the transaction," he said, smiling. His dark eyes locked with hers for a moment, and Tiffany felt as if she'd been given a small and very pleasant shock. The guy was an absolute sex bomb. The flame shapes around the edge of the video screen flared up orange and red.

Sure wouldn't mind meeting him in person, thought Tiffany. "So, okay," she said. "How do we start?"

"That's easy. You just tell me something that you want, and Hot Stuff will get it, or do it for you."

"You've got to be kidding! You mean anything? Anything at all?"

He nodded.

Tiffany snickered. There was no way she was going to believe that. So she said playfully, "Well, then, tell me your name."

He laughed, showing his even white teeth. "People call me Nick. But you don't have to use up one of your Lucky Seven to find that out. Ask for something else."

Downstairs, the hall clock began to chime. Tiffany counted eleven strokes. Bummer! she thought. Past eleven and she still hadn't touched her homework. Normally, she wouldn't have cared. Beavering away at homework wasn't her style. She was smart enough to scrape by doing as little as she could. But it was end of term, and her dad had told her that if she brought home another crummy report card he'd cut off her surfing time. There was no way she wanted that to happen, especially now that she'd found Hot Stuff.

"I want my homework done," she told Nick. "All of it, including that stupid essay I have to turn in tomorrow."

He shrugged. "Okay, if that's what you really want, Tiffany," he said grinning. Then he winked. "Catch you later!"

Tiffany found herself flipped back to her service provider's homepage. She logged off, feeling puzzled. How the heck did Nick know her name? She frowned. Hot Stuff could have planted a cookie on her machine while they were talking. Maybe uploaded some information about who owned the computer. But what about the demonstration she'd asked for? Of course, she knew it was all some kind of a joke. Nick could hardly push her homework through the computer screen, could he? But come on, she hadn't even told him what her homework was!

It was all a scam. It had to be. Still, Tiffany felt a little let down. Then she thought about Nick. Not bad at all, even if he was some kind of con artist. She'd sure like to meet up with him someday! She fell asleep smiling.

The next morning she looked around her room half-expecting to find her completed homework. There was nothing.

Of course there isn't, she scolded herself. How could there be? The guy was just putting you on.

She got to school a little early for once, planning to scribble something down before she had to face her teachers. At the top of the stairs, she saw a folder lying on the floor. Tiffany pounced on it. Annette Tancredi's name was on a label on the front. Inside was a sheaf of paper—Annette's homework. Tiffany thumbed through it quickly. Annette was in every one of Tiffany's classes, and the homework was identical to what she had to hand in that morning.

Well, what do you know? Tiffany thought, grinning. The little grind has made a big fat mistake for once. She glanced around quickly to see if anyone had noticed her pick up the papers. Then she crammed them into her backpack and ducked into the library. There'd be no one there at that hour, for sure.

She riffled through the papers again. Yes, it was all there. Quickly she pulled out some loose-leaf paper and began to copy the first assignment she was due to hand in. The essay was typed, so she wouldn't have to worry about that.

When Mrs. Li came along to collect their assignments in math class, Tiffany handed hers in with a smug smile. A couple of minutes later, she heard voices raised at the back of the room.

"But I *did* do the assignment, Mrs. Li," Annette was pleading.

"I had it in a folder right here in my backpack. I must have dropped it somewhere."

"It isn't like you not to hand in a major assignment, Annette," said Mrs. Li. "I'm sorry, but I have to have a mark for your report card. So I can only give you until the end of the day to turn it in."

Tiffany grinned. Let the silly little grind sweat. It wouldn't hurt her to have a low mark for once, would it? It might even do her good not to be so darn perfect all the time.

Today was turning out just fine after all.

At three o'clock she headed for her locker. Karen Renquist, whose locker was beside hers, shot her a quick sideways glance. "Funny, you having all your homework done today, Tiffany. And Annette losing hers."

"What do you mean?" demanded Tiffany.

Karen tossed her sleek blonde hair. She had a lot of it and liked to flip it about. It always reminded Tiffany that hers was just plain mouse. "Why, nothing. Nothing at all," Karen replied in a singsong voice.

"You better mean nothing!" muttered Tiffany, slamming her locker door. Karen had it all—good looks, great clothes. Friends, too. Everyone noticed *her*. And she always made Tiffany feel like nothing at all. So why couldn't she just mind her own business?

That night she told Nick, "Some demo. You just got lucky. You couldn't possibly do my homework. You didn't even know what it was!"

Nick grinned and shook his head. "No, *you* got lucky, Tiff. I never said I'd *do* your homework. You said you wanted it done.

And it *was* done. By your unfortunate friend. So the Lucky Seven worked, didn't it?"

"She's no friend of mine," Tiffany mumbled. But what she was thinking was, Tiff! He called me Tiff. He must like me!

"So do you want to try Hot Stuff's files tonight, Tiff?" he asked. "Or just go on with the Lucky Seven?"

Maybe she should show some interest. After all, she might want to become a member.

"Sure, I'll check out the files," she said.

"Cool," said Nick. "I'll put you back to hypertext mode, and you can go from there. When you're finished, just click on the Lucky Seven icon." He gave her one of his sexy smiles and disappeared.

Tiffany dipped into the games files. There were lots of them, that was for sure. Every game she'd ever heard of and then some. Most of them were pretty violent, with lots of blood spilled.

"Yuck," she said and clicked on the graphics option. That was even wilder. Murder and mayhem. Sex, too. Made the stuff you saw at the movies seem tame. Amazing how they could show all this kinky stuff on the Internet when movies were restricted.

After a while she lost interest and clicked on Lucky Seven.

"Back already, Tiff?" said Nick. "Didn't care for the files?"

She shrugged.

"Don't worry about that. We have files for every taste. Once you join I'll set up a special program just for you."

Just for her? "I'd love that!" said Tiffany. Nick was really going out of his way to be nice to her. That made her feel pretty special. Somehow she'd never clicked with a guy before. Maybe this could be the start of something. And talk about starting at the top—he was, like, so totally with it. "So what's my next free demonstration?" she wanted to know.

Nick leaned back in his big leather chair. "I keep telling you. Anything you choose."

Oh, sure, thought Tiffany. But she just smiled and said, "Well, I love chocolate. Especially truffles. How about two pounds of truffles?" Let's see him get out of that one! she thought. No one's going to lose a two-pound box of truffles in the school corridor!

For a moment Nick looked just the tiniest bit startled. Then he said, "Let me get this. I'm offering you anything in the whole wide world, and all you want is two pounds of chocolate truffles?"

Tiffany pouted. "That's what I want," she said. "Can't you do it?"

He threw his hands up in the air. "Okay, okay, consider it done," he said, rolling his eyes.

"Uh, Nick?"

"Yeah?"

"Where are you? I mean, do you live anywhere near here?"

"Kid, you know cyberspace. I'm sort of everywhere. I don't even know where you live."

That could be arranged, she thought. "So how are you going to get me my truffles, then?" she asked.

Nick pulled off his cap and ran his hand through his curly black hair. Her fingers itched to do the same thing—his curls looked so shiny and springy.

"Look, Tiff," he said. "I have a large staff. A very large staff. They take care of details like that."

"Oh," said Tiffany. She didn't really understand, but she could see that he was getting bored talking about the subject. Imagine him having a staff working for him at his age. He must be one of those dot-com millionaires! "Well, g'night, Nick," she said softly.

"'Night, Tiff."

There were no chocolate truffles on Tiffany's pillow the next morning, and she didn't find any in the corridors at school. They weren't waiting for her when she got home either. Although she had told herself there was no way she was going to get those truffles, Tiffany still felt disappointed. Despite herself she'd been hoping.

But it was just a scam after all, she told herself. The homework had been a coincidence, just as she'd thought. Wait till she told Nick what she thought of him! In fact, she was rather looking forward to that.

Just before dinner her mother called her down to help out. "We've got company tonight, so put out the best place mats and napkins, and use the silver," her mother told her. "Then come and give me a hand in the kitchen."

"So who's coming?" Tiffany called from the dining room.

"Your Uncle Bob."

"Uncle Bob! Fantastic!" yelped Tiffany. He was her father's kid brother and a real favorite of hers. And so good-looking he was wasted as an uncle.

She heard a quick rap-tap at the front door before it opened. "Hey! Anybody home?"

Tiffany sped to the front hall and hurled herself on her uncle.

She gave him an enormous bear hug and then began to search him. "Okay, where is it?" she demanded.

Her uncle played dumb. "Huh? What are you talking about?"

"Oh, come on. You always bring me something, you know you do," Tiffany replied, digging into his coat pockets. Last time it had been some fabulous DVDs of Japanese rock groups.

"Okay, okay. I surrender," he protested. "Here. Get off me, wild wench!"

From under his overcoat, he pulled out a gift-wrapped box.

Tiffany grabbed it and tore at the wrapping.

"I didn't have much time at the airport, so I had to settle for these," her uncle said. "But I know your sweet tooth. . . ."

"Chocolate truffles," said Tiffany, dazed. "A whole box of them."

"Hey, you're not disappointed, are you? They're Godiva, the very best."

"No, I love them. You're great!" Tiffany hugged him again. Then she stuffed two truffles in her mouth and chewed luxuriously. "Mmmm! They're fantastic!" she mumbled.

Well, Nick, she thought. Guess you got lucky again. Or I did.

She told him so later that night.

"You got your truffles. How doesn't matter, does it?" he said, grinning.

"But . . . but I'd still have gotten them even if I hadn't asked you for them. I mean, Uncle Bob would still have bought them for me."

Nick raised his eyebrows. "Would he?" he asked.

"Aw, c'mon. Are you saying you made him buy them for me?"

"That's one way of putting it."

Tiffany chewed her thumbnail, trying to think of what to ask for next. For some reason she thought of that blonde twit, Karen, and her smart remarks. Then she had an inspiration. She'd show her. And it wouldn't hurt to smarten herself up a little. Maybe Nick would take notice. "Okay. This time I'll ask for something harder. I want to be blonde."

Nick thumped the arm of his chair in exasperation. "There you go again, Tiff, wasting my time. Why don't you just go down to the drugstore and buy some Miss Clairol?"

"Oh, no. I don't want to be phony blonde. I want to be naturally blonde, blonder than Karen Renquist. I want to have been a blonde always, so people don't notice any difference. And," Tiffany paused, thinking of the perfect final touch, "and I want Karen to have my hair color."

Nick rubbed his chin. "Hmmm. You want reality changed. That *is* a bit more interesting. Okay, you're on," he said.

"Really?"

"Sure, Tiff. Wait and see."

Tiffany was suspicious. "Wait? How long?"

"Well, it does take time to tamper with the laws of the universe. Sometime tomorrow probably."

Tiffany finished off the box of truffles to celebrate and went to bed feeling rather sick.

The big change happened between Tiffany's English and History classes the next morning. She'd been peering into mirrors all morning and muttering about Nick and his stupid promises. Then, at five minutes after eleven in the morning, there it was. Her hair was a shimmering golden blonde with eyebrows and eyelashes to match. Even the downy hair on her arms was palest blonde.

Annette Tancredi came into the washroom as Tiffany was preening before the mirror.

"Hi, Annette. Notice anything new about me?" asked Tiffany.

Annette looked her over coolly. "No. Should I?"

Tiffany grinned. "I guess not."

"Why did you do it, Tiffany?"

Tiffany froze and stared at Annette in the mirror. "Do what?"

"You know. Steal my homework and pass it off as yours. I saw that essay you handed in to Mr. Martinelli. It was mine!"

"Go ahead and prove it, then," Tiffany challenged her. "But you can't, can you? Isn't it just too bad!"

"You're a really crummy person, Tiffany Danvers," said Annette, jerking open the door to the hall. "It'll catch up with you one of these days. And when it does it'll serve you right."

"Oh yeah?" Tiffany yelled after her as the door swung shut in her face. She yanked it open again and swaggered out looking for other kids she knew.

Nobody noticed anything different about her. Not even Karen Renquist, who looked pretty mousy with her dull brown hair. She still had cool clothes, but no one gave her a second look now. Tiffany gloated.

She could hardly wait to try her new self on her parents. They weren't home from work when she got back to the house, so she made herself a sandwich and wandered into the living room.

She was about to click on the TV when the family photo

CITY • Of • THE • DEAD

album caught her eye. Okay, here's the final test, she thought.

She flipped open the album and whistled. Tiffany knew perfectly well that she'd been born with brown hair. But here were her parents proudly holding a blonde baby girl. And there she was at her first birthday party—blonde. And the same for the photos of her at Christmas and at dancing class and in all her school photos right up to last year's. She was blonde. Had always been blonde.

But she knew she hadn't!

Well, she thought, this puts a whole new spin on things. Nick really can do big stuff. No way this could be an accident!

Tiffany bubbled with excitement. Why, Nick must think she's crazy! He kept saying she could have anything in the world she wanted, but she'd asked for such stupid things. She felt embarrassed just thinking about it. But everything would be different from now on, she promised herself.

"Money," she told Nick that night. "I want lots and lots of money, so I can buy stuff."

Nick tilted way back in his big chair and grinned at her. "Now, that's more like it. What took you so long?" he asked. "Most people ask for that first."

"Yeah, well, I didn't take you seriously."

"But you do now?" He raised one eyebrow in a totally sexy way.

"I sure do. I mean, you couldn't fake this," Tiffany said, holding up a strand of her silky blonde hair. "By the way, how do you like it?"

"Very fetching," he said. "Though I've always fancied dark-haired chicks myself."

"Oh." Tiffany felt a bit crestfallen. "Well, maybe we'll do that later. When I've gotten tired of this. Now, when do I get rich?"

Nick snapped his fingers. "Just like that," he said. "Money's easy to arrange."

"Aw, c'mon. No way."

"I think you'll find your parents have a little surprise for you," he said. "G'night, Tiff." And he vanished from the screen.

When Tiffany turned around she saw an envelope lying on her desk. She opened it and pulled out a note. A square of plastic slid out of it and landed in front of her.

"Dear Tiffany," the note read. "Your father and I think it's time we gave you more financial independence. You're our only child, after all, so who else should we spend our money on? Go ahead and enjoy yourself. Your loving mother."

Tiffany was stunned. Her mom had written *that*? It was even weirder than getting blonde hair! She picked up the piece of plastic and turned it over. It was a platinum VISA card with her name embossed on the front.

"All right!" she yelled, jumping up and punching her fists at the ceiling. "Look out, mall! Here I come!"

The next night she slouched in front of the computer, dressed from head to foot in gleaming black leather. It looked particularly great with her hair, she thought complacently, as she typed in the URL for Hot Stuff.

"Well?" she demanded as Nick's face appeared.

"Well, what?"

Tiffany scowled at him. Was he blind or something? "Well, don't I look terrific?"

Nick looked a bit startled. Then he grinned. "Yeah, sure you do. Cool. Super-cool."

"That's better," purred Tiffany. Actually, she knew she looked great. The guys at school had been scoping her big time. Everyone except dumb Mike Baur. He was a total hunk, but he was so wrapped up in that little prig Annette that he never glanced at anyone else. What a waste. Hmmm. That gave her an idea.

"Nick," she said, "Here's what I want for my next demonstration. There's this guy at school named Mike Baur. He's in love with Annette Tancredi. Make him love me instead."

Nick frowned. "He really loves her?" he asked.

"Guess so," Tiffany shrugged. "What's the matter? I thought you said I could ask for anything."

"Oh, you can," said Nick. "True love can be tricky to handle, though. I warn you. You may not like what you get. Wouldn't you rather choose something else?"

Tiffany shook her head. "Nope. Just go ahead and do it. I can hardly wait to see that little jerk Annette's face when her lover boy falls at my feet!"

Nick shrugged. "Okay. You've got it," he said. "But it's complicated. It'll have to count as two demonstrations. Agreed?"

Tiffany thought for a moment. Then, "Yeah. It'll be worth it," she said.

The next day at school, Mike came up and asked if he could carry her books. He kept gazing at her in a stunned way, as if he'd never seen her before.

"Sure you can," said Tiffany. "If you'll let me wear your letter jacket."

He looked embarrassed. "Uh, Annette has it," he mumbled.

"So?" said Tiffany. She gazed up into his eyes, and he leaned forward as if hypnotized. She gave him a long clinging kiss. "That's on account," she said. "Now, go get that jacket."

He met her with it between classes, looking miserable. In English, Tiffany made a point of catching Annette's eye. She'd been crying—her eyelids were all red and puffy. Tiffany gave her a big smile and snuggled luxuriously into the jacket.

The other girls glared at her and avoided her after class. She didn't care. She twined her arm through Mike's and paraded down the school corridor. Later, Annette passed them, eyes down, heading the other way. Mike's eyes followed her with a sick look in them.

Tiffany put her lips close to his ear and murmured, "Hey, lover man. Don't you remember who your girl is now?"

He stared at her again, hypnotized. "You, Tiffany. Sure, it's you. All the way." But his eyes slid off to follow Annette out of sight.

Tiffany felt rage boil up inside her. She had Mike, all right, but he was still pining for that sniveling little Annette. It was too much. For the first time she was someone, counted for something. And Annette was ruining everything.

She was still furious that night, and she complained to Nick.

"I warned you," he pointed out.

"Yeah, I know you did. But it really bugs me that she goes around spoiling my fun. I wish she'd drop dead."

Nick gave a low whistle and sat up straight in his chair. "You do?" he asked softly. Flames licked around the edges of the screen.

Tiffany chewed a fingernail. "Yeah, really. I wish she'd fall under a bus or something."

"I'll see to it right away," he promised. "You know, Tiff, you're a pretty amazing girl!" The curling flames around the edge of the screen cast odd shadows on his face for a moment. "Well, g'night Tiff-girl," and disappeared.

Tiff-girl! Tiffany hugged herself with glee. She really was getting somewhere with him, she knew she was. He seemed to think she was his type. Well, goody. She'd practice a bit on Mike, and then . . .

The next day Annette didn't appear in any of their morning classes. By noon the school was buzzing with the news that she had been hit by a bus while crossing a street downtown. She'd died an hour later in the hospital. Tiffany did her best to comfort Mike, but he looked so miserable that she couldn't help feeling a bit sorry for him. She cuddled up against him and his eyes locked onto hers again.

But the whole thing wasn't turning out to be as much fun as she'd thought. Also, she noticed the captain of the football team giving her the eye, and he was even better-looking than Mike. She decided she could afford to give Mike a break. I must be getting soft, she told herself, but it gave her a funny warm feeling all the same. A feeling she couldn't remember ever having had before.

So when she logged on to Hot Stuff that night, the first thing she did was ask Nick to undo her last wish. "Could you, like, bring Annette back to life?" she asked.

He stared out at her, startled. "Don't tell me you repent, Tiff," he said frowning. "I was beginning to think you were my kind of girl. That you'd fit right into my firm."

He wanted her to work for him! Tiffany was ecstatic. There was no way she was going to let him down. "I *am* your type, Nick," she babbled. "Oh, I am. Really I am. No, I'm not a bit sorry. It's just that I've thought of something I'd like better."

Nick shook his head. "Sorry, Tiff-girl. That was the last of your Lucky Seven. So the deal must stand."

"Oh." Tiffany felt a pang of disappointment. Lucky Seven had been the very best thing that had ever happened to her. She'd had more excitement in just a few days than she'd had in her whole boring life. Why did it have to be over? Her eyes brimmed with tears.

"Hey, don't feel bad," Nick told her, grinning. "The good news is that there's absolutely no doubt you qualify for permanent membership in Hot Stuff. In fact, I'd say you're a natural."

Tiffany stared back at him, her eyes widening. Nick's face was blurring and changing. Getting older, uglier. Were those *horns* sprouting from under his baseball cap?

"What do you m-mean, a 'natural'?" she squeaked.

"Why, a natural sinner, of course," Nick replied. Even his voice was different now. Deeper, with a raspy edge to it. "Don't you know you've qualified for the seven deadly sins?"

He began to count them off on his fingers. "You've done sloth—shirking your homework and using someone else's. The truffles? Pure gluttony. Pride and vanity, too—the hair job. And avarice. All those things you wanted from the mall, remember? Then a double dip of envy of Annette and lust for Mike Bauer.

And last but not least, murderous anger. So it's time for you to join our organization. Permanently."

Something in the way he said that last word made Tiffany shiver. "I-I don't want to join!" she quavered, suddenly quite sure that she didn't. "I don't owe you anything—you said it was all free, that I didn't have to pay!"

The face on the screen leaned closer, smiling a terrible smile, and Tiffany shrank back in her chair. "I never said you wouldn't pay for membership in my firm," said Nick. "Just that it wouldn't cost you any money. You accepted our Lucky Seven offer, and now you must join us. A deal is a deal. Too bad, Tiff."

Suddenly, the word *Upload* began to flash at the bottom of the screen in jagged red letters. Tiffany licked her lips. Was it just her imagination, or was the room getting hotter?

Then flames and smoke burst out of the monitor and curled around her. The whole screen imploded, pulling her in and down, down . . .

Somewhere, someone—Nick?—was laughing.

Downstairs, Tiffany's parents heard a shriek, but when they rushed up to her room, they found no trace of her.

Just a fiery point of light dwindling in the center of the monitor. And Tiffany's chair, smoking.

HOOKED

Jamie whipped the casting rod forward, then back, and the line snagged itself on a bush behind him. Muttering under his breath, he put the rod down and started disentangling the line.

He worked it free in a couple of minutes. Then he checked the angle of the sun. It must be after four. Might as well pack it in, he told himself, slapping at a mosquito picnicking on the back of his neck. He'd been working his way upstream for a couple of hours, reading every ripple and rock shadow that seemed to promise fish. But there were no fish, or if there were they sure didn't like the look of his flies.

He wished now that he'd tried a cast or two along the big river lower down the mountain. But there had been such a crowd that he probably wouldn't have caught anything down there either. Up here he'd at least had the stream and the woods to himself— which was the main reason he fished. Not that he'd object to having a fat trout in his creel, he told himself, grinning. Still, it had been a great afternoon. Just being beside running water always unwound something deep inside him. The rod in his hand was really just an excuse. Not that he'd dare tell that to his dad.

Jamie had hiked and fished on most of the mountains around here. But Black Tusk remained his favorite, perhaps because it had never been logged. The forest was old, felt old. All around him the thick trunks of giant evergreens reached upward, the dense canopy of their branches blocking most of the light. The ground was punky with centuries of duff built up by the fallen needles and bark of the trees, and was overgrown with clumps of Oregon grape and salal. Sometimes, when the sun sent shafts of light between the big trees like this, it was like being in church.

He began to untie the fly from the end of his line. It was funny, though, that he'd never found this particular stream before, seeing that it was not far from the main trail up the Tusk. But Jamie wasn't too surprised. Mountains were tricky that way, he knew. Sometimes they showed themselves; sometimes they hid things. That was why he never tired of roaming around up here. Something was different every time.

He stuck the fly carefully in the band of his cap and wound the line back onto the reel. Then he began taking the rod apart. The sun was slanting through the trees on either side of the water. Just the time of day that trout might start rising, he thought. If there were any trout.

A jay shrieked off in the woods somewhere. Then Jamie became aware of a high trilling sound just at the edge of his hearing. It hung on one note for a minute, then fell, then rose again and faded away in a minor key. He stopped for a minute and listened. He'd never heard a bird that sounded like that before.

The sound came again, and again he listened. The woods had

gone very still. There was only the babble of the water and the bird's song. It seemed to be coming from upstream somewhere.

He shouldered his empty creel and turned to go, but the path downstream seemed to have disappeared. Jamie pushed his cap back and scratched his head. Now, wait a minute! It had been a bit overgrown, but he'd had no trouble finding his way along the stream. Was he going crazy or what?

The path leading upstream was clear enough, though. Jamie shrugged. Well, there was no use trying to scramble out through the bushes. He'd follow the path up a way and see if it veered off in the direction of the main trail. Maybe he'd catch a glimpse of the strange bird, too.

He started up the path, which twisted among large boulders and began to climb steeply away from the stream. He turned and looked back down to where he had been casting. There was definitely no sign of a path leading downstream. He'd have to go on up.

The way was narrow and almost overgrown by ferns and creepers in places. Low-hanging evergreen boughs brushed his face, stinging him with their cold spicy smell.

Ahead of him, the strange bird trilled again. And again.

After ten minutes' steady climbing, the path began to curve back toward the stream—he could hear the splash of water just ahead. And then—

"Wow!" he gasped.

The stream had spread out into a large pool. A rocky cliff ran along the opposite side, and at the upper end was a waterfall, where the stream tumbled down in a ribbon of smooth green edged with lacy white.

As he stood there, the bird called again from somewhere near the waterfall. Jamie scanned the trees, but saw nothing and turned back to the pool.

It looked deep. Hunkering down, he stuck his hand into the water. It was icy cold, and he could feel a strong current, scarcely visible on the surface, pushing against the back of his hand.

It had to be the most beautiful place he'd ever seen. And it must be trout heaven.

As if to prove a point, a ripple broke the smooth surface of the water as he watched.

Fish rise! Jamie told himself excitedly. The first action he'd seen all day. He squinted at the sun again. It was getting low. A cloud of gnats was jigging just above the water. Perfect for a trout.

Suddenly, a shining fish broke the surface not six feet away from him. It shot up into the sunlight, snatching a fly before it disappeared back underwater with a flip of its tail.

"Oh, man!" sighed Jamie. "Why didn't I find this place sooner?" His fingers itched to try just one cast. But he knew it was too late. He'd have to go, or he'd never get down off the mountain before dark.

He stood up, slinging his creel over his shoulder. He took a few steps back along the path. The strange bird called again, much closer this time. He glanced wistfully back at the pool, glowing green–gold in the late afternoon light. The sun's rays, slanting between the trees, glinted on the white foam of the waterfall, and for a moment he thought he saw something.

Oh, come on, Jamie thought. He blinked and looked again. It

was gone, whatever it was, the thing that seemed to move and shimmer like a slender body inside the plume of falling water. Just a trick of the light after all.

The path seemed to lead straight out toward the main trail now, though it hadn't looked that way before. Jamie shook his head. It sure was confusing! To make certain he could find his way back again, he dug out his pocket knife and marked small blazes on the trees as he went along. Nothing too obvious—he didn't want to advertise his pool to every yahoo on the mountain.

His pool? Jamie puzzled over the thought. Now, where had that come from? But he did feel that somehow the pool was his. He'd found it, hadn't he?

"Dad?"

"Mmmm?"

Jamie's father was in the den with his nose buried in the business section of the paper. As usual.

"I was up Black Tusk today. Fishing."

His father glanced up. Fishing was the only subject that could get his mind off the stock market for even a minute. "Catch anything?" he asked.

"Nope," admitted Jamie. "Not a single darn fish."

His father grunted. "Thought as much," he said, turning a page of the paper. "It's pretty fished out up there, Jamie."

"Yeah, but I found a neat pool, Dad," Jamie said eagerly. "It's really special. Looks like great fishing."

"So how come you didn't catch anything then?"

"Didn't get a chance. I just stumbled on it when the light was fading and I had to leave. But I saw a trout jump. Rainbow. Nice size. I figure on heading back there next Saturday. Can I have the 4x4 again?"

"Sure, why not?"

Jamie could see that his dad's attention was already drifting back to the TSE Index. "Uh, Dad, maybe you'd like to come along?" he ventured.

His father peered at him over the tops of his glasses. "Well, you go ahead and try it out, and if it amounts to anything let me know. But I've fished every stream and pool on that mountain in my time. There are too many campers and hikers running around up there these days. And every last one of them thinks he has to drop a line, instead of leaving the fish to the real sportsmen."

"Yeah, sure, Dad." Jamie put his ears on hold and turned away. It was his dad's usual rant. Fishing was his religion. He and his pals flew all over North America fly-fishing: Colorado, the Arctic, everywhere. Jamie had begged to be allowed to go with them just once, but his dad kept putting him off, even during the summer holidays when Jamie wouldn't have to miss school.

And now he'd stumbled on a fantastic pool that even his dad didn't know about. Just wait till he came home with a real beauty in his creel. Then his dad would have to pay attention to him.

To Jamie it felt as if the week lasted forever. The thought of the pool on the mountain teased at his mind, and again and again he dreamed of it, of the waterfall and the fish leaping. The strange cry of the bird wove itself in and out of his dreams, too. Each morning he'd wake up smiling.

Just survive until Saturday, my man, he told himself. You can spend the whole day up there. And this time you won't be coming home empty-handed.

But on Saturday morning, Jamie's father took off somewhere in the 4x4 before Jamie could get his hands on it.

Of course my fishing trip isn't important enough for him to remember, Jamie told himself bitterly. Who knows when he'll get back?

He danced around impatiently until his mother took pity on him and let him take her car. Even so, he didn't get to the mountain until a lot later than he'd hoped. He left the car in a parking lot well away from where he was headed and hiked in on a different trail. He hoped he wouldn't meet anyone. He didn't want to lead others to the path he'd blazed if he could help it. Once word got out there was a trout pool not fifteen minutes from the main trail, it would be game over.

Jamie thought of beer cans and plastic bags fouling the clear water and a lot of rowdies spoiling the peace of the place, not to mention scaring the fish. He shuddered.

After a quarter of an hour, he came out on the main trail not far from where he thought he'd marked the side path. But he couldn't see any of his blazes. Puzzled, he stood looking around. Could he have gotten the location wrong?

"Looking for something?"

The gruff voice made Jamie jump. He spun around. An old man with silver hair and a bushy beard was standing on the main trail watching him. A canvas backpack sat on the ground beside him.

Jamie was embarrassed. He must look like a real idiot staring into the bushes. Then he started to get worried. Was the stranger interested in his pool? He didn't seem to have a creel or rod with him.

"Uh, not exactly," he said, hoping the man would lose interest and go on up the trail.

But the man didn't budge. "You wouldn't be looking for a path, would you? A path that leads to a special sort of place?" he asked.

"How do you mean, special?" Jamie hedged. This guy definitely seemed to know something. Maybe the secret pool wasn't so secret after all. He felt a pang of disappointment.

The old man looked amused. "Special like a pool. Don't worry—I'm not a fisherman. Not anymore. It's taken me a lot of years, but I've learned that the best way to enjoy nature is to leave wild creatures alone. And if I were you, I'd stay away from that pool."

He did know about it! "You mean you want to keep it secret," Jamie said flatly. "To protect the fish. But it's on public land, isn't it? And I've got a license."

"It wasn't the fish I was thinking of protecting," the man replied. "Just consider this a friendly warning. Some things are better left alone, that's all. Like that pool you're so interested in. I found my way there once, a long time ago. Lots of great-looking trout. But there's something else there, too."

"Something else?"

"Something you heard up there," the old man said. "Maybe

something you saw, too. Or thought you did."

Jamie thought of what he had glimpsed in the waterfall, but that was nothing. Just a trick of light and shadow. He frowned. "I heard a strange bird singing. That was it."

"Listen. Once I found that pool, I wanted to go back more than anything. It kind of got into my head and ran around there, driving me crazy. But I didn't go back. There was something else there besides fish, you see. I could feel it. I even thought I saw . . . something."

The man shrugged, then went on. "A friend of mine's a Native from the local tribe. When I told him about the pool, he warned me not to go back there. His people knew all about it, you see. Their legends say some pretty strange things have happened there, so they learned to keep away. My friend said it was bad luck to fish there. Very bad luck. He's one smart fella, and I believed him."

Jamie grinned. Native legends? Was that all? "Thanks for the advice," he said. "But I plan to catch me some trout all the same!" He turned away, adding under his breath, "If I can find the darn path, that is!"

It was odd, but no sooner had he spoken the words than he could see one of his blazes on a tree. Right below it, the brown thread of the path wound away through the undergrowth. He followed it in a few steps, then stopped and looked back.

The old guy was shouldering his pack. "Suit yourself, young man," he said. "But remember, you're not the only one who likes fishing."

He waved and headed off up the trail. What the heck was that supposed to mean? Jamie wondered. Of course he wasn't the only one who liked to fish. That was the wonder of the pool—that such a perfect place could exist on a fished-out stream not an hour away from the city. All the more reason to enjoy it while he could. Someone else might stumble across it tomorrow and spoil it. Shaking his head, he followed the path deeper into the woods.

The pool looked just the way he'd been dreaming it. Even better. He stood staring at the shimmering water, lulled by the music of the cascade. Then he gave himself a shake. The place had really taken hold of him, he thought.

By this time the biggest fish would be lurking deep down under those rocky ledges. He'd have to hope they'd find the look of his fly on the surface too tempting to pass up.

The strange bird called once, twice. Almost like a greeting. Jamie whistled back at it, trying to mimic the sound. He dumped his gear and put his rod together, then set about choosing a fly. Maybe he'd try a Royal Coachman. See if that dandy fish he'd seen last weekend would take it for breakfast. Well, brunch.

He cast along the shady side of the pool, letting the fly just kiss the surface and drift down with the current a while before he whipped it into the air again. It was good being there, really good. The sun was warm, but the air was cool from the icy breath of the water.

After a while he began to have a funny feeling, as if he were being watched. Had that old guy followed him in after all? He turned and checked the woods behind him, but there was no sign of anyone. He looked up the pool toward the waterfall. It was deep in shadow.

The trilling cry of the bird wove in and out of the water sound, like an invisible net being cast around him.

Suddenly, he felt a sharp tug on his line. A bite! Delicately, he jerked the line. Not too much, just enough to set the hook. Then he settled back to play the fish, letting it run with the line when it wanted to, then reeling it in a bit when it slowed down.

The fish leaped, breaking the surface in a shower of water-drops. It was a good-sized trout. Maybe the very one he'd seen the other day.

"Oh, you beauty," Jamie said under his breath. Patiently, he let it take the line way out again.

Minutes passed, and he could feel the fish beginning to tire. Gently, he reeled it in until it showed fight again. Then he let it run a bit. At last, when he could see its rainbow sides shining through the clear water, he waded in and scooped it into his net. It really was a beauty, silvery sleek, its sides brushed with rose and green. For a moment something in him wanted to let it go.

"What's the matter with me?" he said. Unhooking the fly from its jaw, he stunned the thrashing fish with a heavy piece of wood and stuffed it into his creel.

The bird gave its weird cry—high, then lower, with the last note falling away.

The sun was high, and he decided to eat his lunch. After he'd finished his sandwiches, he stretched out on the grassy bank in the sun and pulled his cap down over his eyes. No need to hurry. There'd be plenty of time to try his luck again later. It felt good to be here beside the pool. As if he belonged here somehow.

Sleep closed over him, and he began to dream uneasily. The trilling of the bird mingled with the sound of the waterfall, pulling him deeper and deeper.

He was under the water, looking up at ripples on the surface. Then something loomed at the edge of his field of vision. It was a huge fish, much bigger than the trout he'd caught. At least, he thought it was a fish. Most of its slender body was lost in shadow and a cloud of something silvery-looking drifted around it. Through the cloud, its eyes stared at him, round and expressionless. He wanted it to come closer, yet as it moved toward him he felt a sense of dread.

A loud splash in the pool woke him. Jamie sat up and looked around. Ripples were spreading across the surface as if something big had jumped.

The angle of the sun surprised him. He must have slept longer than he'd intended.

He was hot and felt a bit dizzy, as if he'd gotten too much sun. The water looked so cool, so inviting that Jamie stripped and waded in. He ducked under the surface and shot up again with a yell at how bone cold the water was. The sound echoed and re-echoed off the face of the cliff, then died away among the trees. He trod water, listening, shocked at the noise he'd made.

He submerged again and this time the water didn't seem so cold. He opened his eyes, looking up. But that made him think uneasily of his dream. So he rose to the surface and floated on his back, sculling lazily with his arms. The sun was hot on his face, the current flowing satin cold against his back. Then a cloud drifted across the sun and he felt the touch of its shadow pass the length of his body. It seemed to him that he had never felt sun and shade and water so intensely before.

At last the chill of the water began to seep into him, so he swam back a few strokes, then stood up and waded toward the bank. Suddenly, something cold and strong wrapped itself around his legs and pulled him under. Choking on a mouthful of water, he struggled and thrashed his way on all fours through the shallows, the stones on the bottom cutting into his knees. He hauled himself onto the bank and lay there, gasping. After a moment, he rolled over on his back and sat up.

The ripples from his passage had disappeared, and the surface of the pool was undisturbed. Well, what was he expecting to see? He must have tripped over his own feet and then panicked, that was all. But he didn't really believe that. It was as if the skin of his legs had memory and could still feel the touch of something cold and slippery smooth wrapped around them. Like, like—*arms?*

The sound of the waterfall was loud in his ears, the water chuckling to itself as it plunged over the rocks. He'd never thought of the sound that way before—like laughter. Narrowing his eyes, he stared at it. The sun was striking the cascade at an angle now. The water flowed down green and smooth, grooved in the middle like a long bare back. And the white water at the edges looked almost like silvery hair.

Something moved inside the water . . . or did it?

"Hey!" yelled Jamie. Then felt stupid standing there shouting at a waterfall. But he'd thought he saw something there the last time, too. And hadn't the old man said he saw something in the water?

Jamie didn't feel like fishing anymore. He started to dismantle his rod. Then he heard another splash in the pool behind him. Ripples were spreading.

Fish rise? he wondered, squinting up at the sun. It was still pretty early for that. But something was going on in the pool. He put the rod down and waded into the water. When it was up to his waist, he took a deep breath and squatted down, opening his eyes. He saw nothing except a few minnows darting among the rocks at the edge of the pool. Then, just as in his dream, something shadowy loomed before him. Something large. His lungs nearly bursting, he waited. Either it was the biggest fish he'd ever imagined, or . . . But what else could it be?

Whatever it was drifted nearer, always keeping to the shadows. Then he saw . . . he thought he saw . . . a face with staring eyes. Cold amber eyes in a strange flat face with long silvery hair floating all around, a face with a wide lipless mouth that smiled, baring needle-sharp teeth. It was there for only a second, then it vanished into the shadows under the bank.

It was the creature in his dream—except he wasn't dreaming now!

Jamie shot up out of the water, gasping for breath, and backed toward the shore. Despite the warmth of the sun on his wet skin, he was shivering as he struggled into his clothes. The weird bird called again, from very near. If it *was* a bird. He wasn't sure of anything now.

Grabbing his creel and his rod, Jamie scrambled for the path. He couldn't find it. Cursing, he struggled through the bushes in the direction he thought it would be. Then the bird called again, and the path was simply there, right before him.

Jamie sneaked into the kitchen and set his creel on the counter. Unhooking the wicker lid, he stared at the fat trout curled inside it on a bed of fern fronds. He'd almost been tempted to toss it away on the mountain, but somehow the farther away he got from the pool, the sillier that had seemed. It was a great fish, wasn't it? The best he'd ever caught. It was stupid to get upset because he imagined he'd felt and seen something in the pool. He must have had a touch of sunstroke, that was all. Still, he didn't think he'd be eating the fish. Something about its eyes bothered him. Even in death they seemed to be trying to tell him something.

"Jamie?" His father was calling him from the den.

Quickly, almost guiltily, Jamie flipped the creel shut and turned around, trying to block it from sight. If his dad saw it . . . So what if he does? he thought, puzzled. I want him to see I was right, don't I?

"Thought I heard you," his father said, coming into the kitchen. "Jamie, I'm sorry I took off in the 4x4 this morning. I completely forgot you had fishing plans—it never crossed my mind until I was all the way downtown. Did you make it up Black Tusk all right?"

"Yeah. Yeah, I did. Mom lent me her car."

"And? How did the pool pan out?"

Jamie shrugged. "Okay, I guess," he said.

His father glanced at the creel. "Got a fish in there?"

"Yeah. But it's nothing special."

"I told you you wouldn't catch anything much up there," his father reminded him. He strolled over and flipped up the lid of the creel. Then he whistled. "You call *this* nothing special?" he asked. "Why, it must be at least twelve pounds!"

Jamie shrugged. "There are probably bigger ones," he mumbled. He could have bitten his tongue.

His father's eyes lit up with an unholy gleam. "You mean there are more where this came from? I can't believe it—who'd have thought there was anything like this left on the Tusk! You'll have to take me up and show me."

"I dunno, Dad," Jamie began. One part of him wanted to show his dad he'd been wrong about the Tusk, prove that he knew a good place when he saw one. But another part didn't want to go back to the pool. Not with his father. Not with anybody.

To his surprise, his dad put his hand on his shoulder. "Come on, Jamie," he said. "I know how you feel, not wanting to share a good thing. You've turned out to be quite a fisherman after all, haven't you? A real chip off the old block."

Jamie stared glumly down at the toes of his hiking boots.

His dad cleared his throat. "Look, Jamie," he went on. "When I remembered about your fishing trip this morning, it made me feel pretty bad. It made me think about a lot of other things, too. You asked me to go with you last week, and I wouldn't. That wasn't very nice of me. I know I don't make enough time for us to do things together." He shrugged. "Guess I'm just a one-track kind of guy. I get so caught up in things at the office that it's hard for me to try a new direction."

He waited for a moment, but when Jamie still said nothing, he added, "Anyway, why not make a fresh start now, son? Let's go up the Tusk tomorrow, just the two of us. The way you invited me last week. You can show me your pool. From the looks of things, you have plenty to show."

Jamie didn't know what to say. Here was his dad offering to spend time with him one-on-one, just as he'd always wanted. But—go back to the pool? A prickly kind of instinct told him it was better not to. "M-maybe it's not such a good place to fish after all, Dad," he faltered. "An old guy I met on the trail today even warned me not to fish there. It's hard to explain. There *is* something funny about the pool."

The excuse sounded lame, even to him.

"Something fishy, you mean?" his father asked, grinning. Then his expression grew serious. "I don't blame you for holding out on me, son," he said. "I deserve it. But give me a chance to make things up to you. I swear I won't tell another soul about your pool, if that will make you feel better. And Jamie? You know that trip up country I'm planning for this fall? Maybe you could come along. You're old enough to fit in now and pull your weight. Of course, you'd have to miss a bit of school, but we could work that out. What do you say? Is it a deal?"

He stuck out his hand.

Jamie swallowed hard. His dad really seemed to mean it about making a fresh start. And to go along on one of his fabulous trips would be a dream come true. Flying into remote lakes in a chartered plane. Camping out in style with fishing guides and all. Wait till he told the guys at school!

He hesitated a moment longer, remembering round staring eyes. Fish eyes. But he chased the thought away. "Sure, Dad, it's a deal," he said, shaking hands.

That night Jamie didn't sleep well. Rain set in, thrumming on the roof over his head. He dreamed he was back at the pool. He saw the fish jump again. Then he was under the water himself, swimming. The trilling of the strange bird wove itself through the dream.

He woke while it was still dark and tossed restlessly, knowing that the pool was up there waiting for him. He was sitting on his bed, ready, when his father tapped on his door at four o'clock.

It was raining when they left, though it tapered off as they drove up the mountain. But the sky remained leaden, and clouds clung low on the heights of Black Tusk.

Jamie's father was pleased. "Great fishing weather," he said, as they got their rods and creels out of the back of the 4x4. "Maybe it'll rain again if we're lucky. That should make the big ones rise."

Nobody else was in the parking lot, and the trails were deserted. The woods were dark and dripping, with a clammy mist curling between the trees.

"How far up did you say it was?" his father asked as they started up the trail.

"Not far," said Jamie.

They climbed quickly in silence. Jamie had thought he didn't want to go back to the pool. Yet the closer he got to it, the more he needed to be there. It was almost as if something was tugging at him.

What if he couldn't find the path this time? The thought nagged at him, and he walked even faster.

After a quarter of an hour they were near to where the path branched off.

"The path should be around here somewhere," said Jamie.

"Didn't you blaze it?"

"Sure I did!" replied Jamie. How could he explain a path that appeared and disappeared whenever it felt like it?

Just then his father stopped and pointed. "Over there, Jamie. Is that one of your blazes?"

"Yeah, I think so," said Jamie.

They left the main trail and tramped in, getting drenched as branches dripped water down the backs of their necks. Jamie could hear the waterfall now. Today it didn't sound like laughter. Its voice was a sullen growl.

His father heard it, too. "Sounds like there's a lot of runoff from the rain," he said.

They broke out of the woods at the edge of the pool. It was the color of dull silver under the leaden sky, the waterfall a swollen torrent of gray and white.

"Good God!" Jamie's father said, taking it in. He turned to Jamie. "You were one hundred percent right, son. What an incredible pool! I've never seen the like, not even in Scotland. And to think it's right here practically under my nose. I really do owe you one for this!"

The strange bird called.

"What's that bird, dad?" Jamie asked.

"Huh?" His father looked up from putting his rod together. "I didn't hear anything."

Jamie left his father to cast from the bank where he'd fished before and moved upstream closer to the waterfall. He whipped his rod back and forth, but he wasn't really fishing. He was keeping an eye on what his father was doing.

Hope he catches something quickly, he thought. Now that he was back at the pool, he felt uneasy. Even with his father there he had the same feeling of being watched as he'd had the day before. He glanced up at the waterfall. Something was hiding in that water or in the depths of the pool below. He could feel it. He remembered long weedy hair adrift on the current, cold clinging arms. Not an it, he realized, with a sharp intake of breath. A *she*. But whatever *she* was, she wasn't going to show herself, not with both of them there.

Jamie shivered and flicked his line listlessly over the water. He really didn't feel like fishing.

Ten minutes later, his father let out a whoop that nearly made him drop his rod. There was something on his dad's line, and from the bend in the rod, it looked big.

Jamie reeled in his own line and ran down the bank.

His father was letting out line as the fish ran with it.

"Incredible!" his father said between clenched teeth. "You weren't kidding about there being big ones left! This must be a whopper!"

It took half an hour before the fish gave up and came close enough to be netted. Jamie's father stunned it and hooked his fingers through its gills. He held it up, grinning fiercely. "Yes!" he breathed. Then he stowed the fish carefully in the creel and sat down on a log and poured himself a coffee from the thermos they'd brought. "Your turn, son. Don't mind saying I need a breather after that," he admitted, shaking his head.

Jamie picked up his rod and walked slowly back toward the waterfall. He hesitated, but his father was watching and gave him the thumbs-up signal. So he checked the fly on his line and cast. The moment the fly touched the surface, something seized it and dove with it. Jamie's throat felt choked with excitement and fear. He started playing out the line, hoping the fish on the end of it would throw the hook or that the line would part. But his finger tangled in the filament, and the rod bent in a dangerous arc.

"Jamie! Pay out more line!" his father yelled. "The rod will snap!"

Jamie yanked his finger free, and the line shot out of the reel with a whizz. The fish headed straight down the pool, as if trying to reach the shelter of the rocky ledges at the foot of the cliff. Then, unable to shake the hook, it swerved back. Jamie's hands seemed to take on a life of their own, reeling in frantically to keep the line from tangling. Right below the waterfall, the fish hurled itself into the air, trying to shake off the agony of the hook in its mouth. It danced across the water on its tail before plunging beneath the surface.

It was the biggest fish Jamie had ever seen. Numbly, he went on playing it, paying out more line.

His father was running toward him along the bank, yelling something, but Jamie couldn't hear him. He felt cold and hot at the same time, as if electricity were jolting into him through the bending rod. Dimly, he was aware of his father beside him, urging him on.

It felt as if the struggle would go on forever, but at last he could feel the spirit going out of the fish. Its leaps and lunges became shorter, and at last it swam quietly, only the current tugging at the line. Little by little Jamie reeled it close enough to net. Except that it was too big to fit into the net.

Jamie's father waded into the shallows to help land the fish. "What a monster!" he yelled. Using the net as a scoop, he managed to heave it up on the bank.

Jamie watched the huge fish thrash. The electric feeling had gone now, leaving him cold and sick. I wish I hadn't caught it, he thought.

"Stun it, Jamie!" his father shouted, clambering up the bank. "It's getting close to the edge."

But Jamie stood frozen, the roar of the waterfall loud in his ears. His father grabbed a piece of wood and clubbed the fish. It took several blows to kill it.

Then he ran down to his creel and got a pocket scale. He hooked it through the jaw of the fish and hoisted it. "It's right off the scale, Jamie," he said in an awed voice. "Way bigger than mine, if you can believe it! You must have caught the king of the pool!"

Jamie watched the rainbows fading on the sides of the huge fish. Its dead eyes stared up at him, and he felt a wave of pity tinged with fear.

"What a trophy!" his father exclaimed. "I've never caught anything like this. Just wait till I get it mounted for you."

Around them, the dark woods watched and listened, and the waterfall sang its angry song. Then the rain began to pour down in a steady sheet.

His father glanced up at the clouds, which were closing down around the treetops. "Guess that's enough for today," he said. "We couldn't do better than we've already done, that's for sure!"

Jamie took the rods apart while his father got out his knife and cleaned the fish. As the guts slid into the water, Jamie felt a twinge in his own belly, and his stomach turned over.

What's the matter with me? he wondered.

"We'll be back," his father promised as they turned away from the pool. "Soon."

Over the roar of the waterfall, Jamie heard the bird cry once, thin and high.

His father was still celebrating as they slogged back down the main trail. "I can't wait to see the guys' faces when they see that fish of yours," he said. "They'll never believe you caught it right here on Black Tusk, but I'm your witness." Then he added, "Son, I'm proud of you. I thought I knew it all, but you've proved me wrong, and I'm glad to admit it."

Jamie stopped in his tracks and stared at his father, rain trickling down his face. "Dad, you're not going to tell your friends where I caught it, are you?" he protested. "You promised! You said you'd keep the pool a secret. Just between the two of us, you said."

His father's face fell. "Aw, Jamie. Can't I just tell one, maybe two? Can't I even brag about my own son once in a while? Anyway, that big fellow you caught was the king of the pool— must be. So nobody's going to be able to top you!"

"I don't care about that!" snapped Jamie. He jogged down the path ahead of his father.

"Jamie? What's the matter?" his father called after him.

Jamie didn't answer.

That's it, then, he thought to himself as they clambered into the 4x4. Even if his dad only told one or two guys they'd be bound to tell others. They'd fish out the pool. And with all of their comings and goings, it wouldn't be long before more people noticed and began going there, too. The pool would be ruined, and she would be destroyed, too. Surely even her wild magic couldn't stand up to all that.

He shivered. The old man on the trail had been right. Some places were better left alone.

Still, as soon as they left the clinging mists of the mountain behind he began to feel better. It was out of his hands now. There was nothing he could do about anything, he reminded himself. And he'd caught a fantastic fish, though he hadn't really wanted to. Now, if only he could stop remembering the way its eyes looked.

His dad reached over and patted his knee. "Fine fishing pool, son. And a great day's catch. I owe you one. You can count on that trip this fall."

The trip! Jamie managed to smile back at his father. "Sure, Dad. That'll be great," he said.

He lay awake for a long time that night. The chuckling of the rain in the downspout outside his window reminded him of the waterfall. When he did sleep, he dreamed of being underwater again, with the strange singing in his ears and an ominous shadow swimming toward him.

When he woke the next morning, it was still raining. Jamie squelched off to school through the downpour. His head felt heavy, and he found it hard to think straight. The only good part of the day was swimming practice last period. The water felt great, and he made such terrific time on his heats that the coach gaped at him in surprise. The only thing was, every time he put his head underwater he kept expecting to see something.

But when he got out of the pool, he didn't feel so good. Even after he showered, his skin felt itchy. And the back of his throat tickled.

"Must be the chlorine," he told himself.

He could hardly eat dinner that night. He was finding it hard to swallow, and he felt short of breath. There were funny noises in his head, too. He must have got a lot of water in his ears.

"Jamie?" His mother's voice had an edge of worry to it.

"Huh? I mean, pardon, Mom?"

"You look awful. I asked if you were feeling all right," she said.

"Not so hot. I must have caught a cold out in the rain yesterday."

His mother sighed. "Men!" she said.

His father gave him a broad wink. "But it was worth it, eh? It's not every day you get to catch the king of the pool."

Jamie nodded. The pool . . . yes, the pool, he thought dizzily.

His mother told him to go to bed early and he didn't protest. Lying in the dark, he thought only of the pool. The pool and what was in it. The rain drummed steadily on the roof just over his head, and he thought he could hear a far-off voice calling.

He got up and padded down the hall to the bathroom to splash his hot face. He stood there for a long time, half-hypnotized, watching the stream of water from the faucet swirling down the drain. Water. *Waterwaterwater . . .*

When he slept at last, he found himself back in the depths of the pool. And that face with the needle teeth coming nearer.

He woke up thrashing, half suffocating. His skin prickled as if thousands of tiny knives were poking through it. His throat felt parched, as if he had been breathing through his mouth. He reached for the glass on the bedside table and swallowed the water in it in one gulp. Still thirsty, he climbed out of bed and went to the bathroom to get more.

He closed the bathroom door quietly and turned on the light. He filled the tumbler and drank. As he filled it again, he glanced into the mirror. The glass dropped from his nerveless fingers and shattered in the sink.

His face was covered with some kind of a rash. It was on the backs of his hands, too. He must be coming down with some weird disease! Through the water noise in his head he tried to think. Measles? Couldn't be. He'd had measles. All sorts of measles. Chicken pox, too. So what was it?

He touched his face with his fingertips. It felt rough. Feeling sick to his stomach, he turned off the light and stumbled back to bed.

He awoke with the first gray light of morning, his mouth wide open, his throat painfully dry. He sat up and looked at the backs of his hands, hoping the rash was better. It wasn't. In fact, it looked worse, and his skin was crusted with shiny little ridges. Shrinkingly, Jamie touched the back of one hand. It felt—he tried to swallow—scaly.

A wave of nausea rushed over him. Trying to catch his breath, he opened and closed his mouth, gasping, but the air seemed to burn his throat. Then he noticed a strange sensation. Trembling, he felt behind his ears. He could feel ridges there, too. Long ones, like scars. Then they gaped open under his fingers! Horrified, he snatched his hands away. They were slits, not scars, slits opening and closing in the sides of his head. *Gills!*

The water sound was louder in his ears. It was all around him now, a singing mixed with laughter. Gloating laughter. The thing in the pool was calling him and laughing at him because she knew he'd have to come.

You're not the only one who likes fishing.

The old man on the trail had warned him, but he hadn't listened. Jamie understood it all now. The thing in the pool had lured him that very first day—with her strange song, with her fish, with a glimpse of herself. Then she'd played him, making sure he couldn't stay away. Teasing him, letting him think he was running free, but reeling him in little by little with her song in his dreams.

"Fishing," he mumbled through thickening lips. And he had taken the bait. Now she'd hooked him.

He thought of the cold deep water of the pool, and his body cried out for it. He could hardly get his breath now. He had to get to the pool! *Hurryhurry* . . .

He threw off the covers and dragged on his clothes. When he was dressed, he tiptoed downstairs and found the keys to the 4x4. He opened the kitchen door. It was blowing rain outside, and the drops felt sweet as kisses on his tortured skin.

But he couldn't just leave like this. He tore a piece of paper from a pad and found a pencil. His fingers felt strangely stiff now, and it was hard for him to hold it. Awkwardly, he scrawled a couple of words. It was all he could manage. He left the note on the kitchen table and stumbled out the open door.

He let the car roll down the driveway before he started the engine. Traffic was light, and he was up the mountain in less than half an hour.

The dark woods dripped around him as he panted up the path, mist curling about his feet. *Hurryhurry . . .*

Long before he reached the pool, he heard the roar of the waterfall and the singing in it. The water was a dark mirror, the waterfall black and tasseled with silver. He tore off his clothes and stood on the bank for a moment, turning his face up to the rain, letting it sluice off the edges of his scales.

The water song and laughter in his head made it hard to think. He knew only that he needed the water. The air burned in his tender new gills, and with a gasp of relief, he plunged into the pool.

She was waiting.

Why? Jamie wondered, before he thought no more.

In her round deep eyes he read the answer. She was lonely.

And now there was a new king of the pool.

Down in the city, the wet wind gusted through the kitchen. It caught the note and sent it fluttering to the floor. Water claimed it, soaking the paper, dissolving the clumsily scrawled words:

"GONE FISHING."

FLYING·TOASTERS

Denise keyed in the remote connection. She found the file she was looking for and clicked Download. When the screen flashed "Transfer Completed," she surfed back to her service provider. The file was in her mailbox. She downloaded it to her home machine and ran a standard virus check. The file was clean, so she transferred it into her exec.directory. Now the computer would run it every time she turned it on.

The phone rang. She picked it up, cradling it in her shoulder. It was Mike Franklin, her boyfriend.

"Yo, Mike," she said. "Yeah, I got it. It hasn't run yet. Should come up on-screen any minute now."

Suddenly, tiny pink gizmos with blue wings flapped across the screen. They looked kind of like toasters, Denny thought. Some of them chugged straight ahead while others flipped over, reversed direction or crashed into each other.

Denise chuckled. "Hey, it works," she said into the phone. "Crazy toasters. And there are supposed to be plenty of other images, too. I can't wait to see the look on Mom's face. Well, see you tomorrow. Bye."

Denny saw quite a lot of the toasters the next afternoon because she was trying to do an English assignment and couldn't think of anything to write. It was funny how she felt kind of happy and peaceful watching the toasters.

Around five, her mother got home from work, having picked up Grub, Denny's little brother, from day care. Her mother called hello, and a moment later she appeared in the doorway carrying Grub. She put him down. "Would you keep an eye on the monster child while I get changed?" Then she saw the screen. "What on earth are those?" she asked, walking across to stare at the display. Grub toddled after her.

Denny looked up at her, grinning. "New kind of screensaver," she said. "Yo, Grubster," she added as he clambered into her lap.

Grub pointed at the computer screen. "Iss?" he wanted to know.

"Toasters, Grub," said Denny, grinning. "Flying toasters."

"'Oasers," he repeated.

"What will the nerds come up with next?" her mother said, shaking her head.

Denny shrugged. "Nothing new about screensavers. But this one's supposed to be some big-deal upgrade. I had to go all over the Net to find it."

Her mother shook her head. "I don't know how you kids pick up all this stuff."

"Born wired, I guess," said Denny smugly.

"Well, look at that?" her mother said, glancing down at Grub. "Usually, he's completely wild by the afternoon," she went on. "Eileen at the day care said he's been tearing the place apart."

After staring blissfully at the screen for a couple of minutes, Grub had gone to sleep with his thumb in his mouth.

"Miracles do happen," Denny said, as her mother tiptoed away.

Denny hitched herself closer to the computer, shifting Grub across her lap. She really had to make a start on that essay.

It wasn't until later that night that she noticed anything odd. She'd left the computer on while she ate supper and came back to find the toasters on the screen. She settled in and went to work on the essay. After an hour, she had to stop. Something was distracting her. As if some movement was going on just outside her field of vision. She looked around. Nothing. She started working, and in a moment she had the same sensation again.

Denny looked over her shoulder, and there it was. A tiny toaster. It was flapping slowly through the air just about eye level, but off to one side.

"Whoa!" she said, closing her eyes. When she opened them the toaster was still there. As she watched, another one plinked into existence and then another. She stared, openmouthed, while the toasters bumped into each other and set off in separate directions.

Denny giggled. "Boy, I'm seein' things!" she said. "I'm for bed." She got up and switched off the computer. The toasters vanished.

Well, of course they did, she told herself. They were never there!

She told Mike about it at school the next day. He grinned. "You're loopy, girl," he told her.

"Guess I was just tired," she admitted.

When she got home, she smelled peanut butter cookies and

followed her nose to the kitchen. Her mother was just removing them from the oven. She was wearing jeans and a sloppy sweatshirt, and her hair was in a messy ponytail.

"Wow!" Denny said, reaching for a cookie. "It's a supermom attack!"

"It happens," said her mother, looking sheepish. "Hey, be careful. Those are still hot." She started putting the cookies on a rack to cool. "I worked at home today. Big policy paper for the minister. I got it all done, and then, oh, I don't know. . . ."

"Mothering just sneaked up and ambushed you," finished Denny, juggling a hot cookie. "Hey, no problem. I love it!" She looked around. "Where's Grub?"

"Under the table. He's been some kind of animal all day. A bear, I think."

Denny checked under the table. "Excuse me, but he's not here," she reported.

"Oh, my lord," wailed her mother. "He's faster than lightning! I left the computer on. If he gets at it or into my papers . . ."

"I'll find him," said Denny, charging back down the hall.

She didn't have to go far. Grub was sitting on the floor of the den. He beamed at her as she appeared in the doorway. "'Oasers," he said, pointing at the bookcase. Sure enough, a covey of flying toasters was flapping along one of the shelves.

"I don't believe this," Denny said. She called back down the hall, "It's okay, Mom." Then she shut the door. If Mom sees this, she'll go ballistic, she thought, watching the toasters loop the loop in formation.

She hit Save, then keyed in the commands to exit the word

processing program. Then she switched the computer off and looked around.

No toasters.

Grub crinkled up his face and got ready to howl.

"Hold on, Grubbie," Denny said, turning the computer on again. After a minute, the toasters reappeared on the screen. Not long after, the first one plinked into view over Grub's head. He chuckled, pleased.

Swell, Denny said to herself. Now what? She reached for the phone. When Mike answered, she said, "You've got to come over. I need to show you something."

"Now?" he protested. "It's suppertime, and Mom's having lasagna."

"Forget your stomach," she said. "Tell your mom you're having supper here. Just get over here! Fast!"

Mike sighed. "Okay, okay. Chill out, will you, Denny?"

The intercom buzzed ten minutes later.

"It's okay about dinner," Denny told him as she let him into the apartment. "I told Mom we have to work on a project together."

"As long as you feed me," he said.

"Here, take this," she replied, stuffing a peanut butter cookie in his mouth. Then she dragged him into the den and shut the door behind them.

"Now, what do you think of that?" she demanded, pointing.

Grub, who had refused to be parted from the toasters, pointed, too, grinning.

The air was full of them now.

"Mmnf!" Mike nearly choked on his cookie.

Denny folded her arms. "Is that all you have to say?"

Mike sank down on the computer chair. First he looked at the toasters on the screen, then at the ones in the air.

"I didn't see nearly this many before," Denny told him. "But Mom's had the computer on all day."

"So turn it off," said Mike.

"I tried that, dummy. They just come back when you switch it on again."

"Oh. Well, there's something screwy about this. Better delete it from the memory."

They brought the contents of the exec.directory up on-screen.

"It isn't there!" yelped Denny.

"Are you sure this is where you put it?" asked Mike.

"Sure I'm sure. How else would the program run?" demanded Denny.

"Yeah, well, it's not there now. Let's try Find File," he suggested. "What's the name of it?"

"ScreenTastic," said Denny.

"NO FILE FOUND," read the screen.

"So much for that," said Michael, scratching his head. "There must be something screwy in the 'ware itself. Didn't you run a virus scan on it?"

"Of course I did!" Denny was indignant. "How dumb do you think I am?"

"Okay, okay. Let me think," he said, sitting back and staring at the screen.

After a minute the toasters reappeared. Soon Mike and Denny

were sitting in the middle of a large swarm of them. Mike waved his hand through them. They seemed to go right through him.

Mike chuckled. "They tickled a bit," he said. "Like a very faint electric shock." He watched the toasters for a few moments, then turned to Denny, grinning. "You know, I kind of like them," he admitted.

"I know what you mean," said Denny. "They make you feel sort of . . . peaceful."

"Why get rid of them, then?"

"Are you kidding?" said Denny. "Mom will have a fit if she sees them. She'll get right on my case about messing up her new computer."

"Okay, okay. But let's leave it until after dinner," Mike bargained. "Keep the door closed so your mom doesn't see them."

Denny nodded and picked up Grub. "More toasters later," she promised him. "After supper."

"'Oasers funny," Grub chortled.

"You bet," Mike agreed, switching the light off and closing the door behind them.

The toasters had disappeared when they got back after supper. Instead, raindrops were falling soundlessly on the computer screen and slanting through the room.

"What now?" demanded Mike.

Denny slammed the door shut and leaned against it. "I bet it's Pitter Patter."

"Huh?"

"There were other settings besides the toasters. Pitter Patter. Bouncing Nerds. Who knows what else?"

"You mean this thing is resetting itself as well as running around inside the drive?"

Denny nodded. "Looks like it."

Mike slumped down in the computer chair and scowled at the screen. Pitter-pats of electronic rain beat down on him. After a few minutes he stopped scowling and stretched. "Jeez, I feel so relaxed," he said yawning. "No use getting ourselves all upset about this. What harm is it doing?"

Denny dragged him out of the chair. "Get away from that screen. I've already got one addict in the family. Grub and his 'oasers. Not you, too!" She pushed him into the hall and closed the door behind them.

After a moment he blinked and said, "Yeah, guess we'd better do something. But it's way beyond me. There's only one guy who might know what to do."

Denny gasped. "You mean—"

"Yeah. Meganerd."

"Oh, come on Mike. Alex Bates won't pay any attention to us. He thinks we're cretins."

"Well, compared to him we *are* cretins," said Mike, picking up the hall phone and dialing. "Yo, Alex?" he said a moment later. "It's Mike Franklin. Yeah, I know you're busy, so I'll give it to you quick. Heard anything about that hot new screensaver program out of HSL Labs? Yeah, Denny and I did, too. Well, she downloaded it. And guess what? We've got virtual flying toasters."

Leaning over his shoulder, Denny heard a kind of muffled squawk.

"Yep, virtual," Mike went on. "Swarms of them flying all

around the room. Not to mention electronic raindrops falling on our heads."

"*Squawk, squawk,*" went the phone.

"Yeah, we tried all that. The darn thing has exited the exec.directory. We can't find it. And it's resetting itself. Yeah, I agree. Must be some weird virus."

Denny grabbed the receiver. "Alex? Denny. Listen, you gotta help us. My mom will ground me for life if she finds out I've screwed up her new computer."

"Uh, hi, Denny," said Alex. "Okay. Lemme think." There was a moment's silence before he went on. "Your virus disinfectant's probably out of date. I know a guy at U Chicago who's up on all the latest weird stuff out there. Let me see if I can download something from him and put it on a disk. Shouldn't take long."

"We can come pick it up," offered Denny.

"Nah, I'll bring it over," Alex said. "Virtual toasters I gotta see!"

"Well, if you're like everyone else around here, you'll love 'em," said Denny and hung up. "Gee," she said to Mike. "He's actually coming over."

Mike shrugged. "Only because it's something to do with computers."

The buzzer went off forty minutes later.

"I'll get it, Mom," yelled Denny, heading for the intercom. "Just someone else who's working on the project."

Her mother peered at her over the back of the couch. "Another one? How many does it take?"

Alex looked as if he hadn't slept for a week. His hair was

uncombed, and his glasses needed cleaning. He wore a short-
sleeved shirt with ballpoint pens in the breast pocket. "Here
y'are," he said holding out a disk. "Now, show me."

"In there," said Denny, pointing him toward the den.

They found Mike in front of the computer again, peacefully
watching electronic raindrops falling on the screen. They were all
around him, too.

"Way cool," said Alex, waving his hand through the image
field.

"Yo, Meganerd," said Mike, grinning. "Howza boy?"

Alex turned to Denny. "Is Franklin on something?"

"They kind of make you feel good," Denny ventured. "Sort
of relaxed. My little brother absolutely loves them. The flying
toasters, that is."

"Hmmm." Alex looked thoughtful. His glasses had slid down
his nose, and he pushed them up with one finger. "Well, let's see
what this disinfectant will do," he said. "Move your butt,
Franklin," he added, yanking the chair out from under him.

Alex hitched the chair closer to the computer and put the disk
in the disk drive. His fingers danced over the keys as he saved it
into the exec.directory and then ran it.

"Chicago guy says this should kill off just about any known
Trojan Horses and viruses," he said over his shoulder. "Of
course, it's all through your computer now."

"Swell," groaned Denny, trying to calculate how many years of
her allowance it would take to buy her mother a new computer.

"No Viruses Detected," read the screen.

"Oh yeah?" said Mike, grinning.

"I'll try Reset," said Alex, hitting another command.

The onscreen images died, and the raindrops disappeared from the air.

Denny cheered as the screen returned to normal. A minute later, she fell silent as the screen filled with images again. This time it was weird little guys on pogo sticks.

Mike snickered. "Bouncing Nerds, I presume," he said.

Pretty soon the air was full of them. Denny shot a glance at Alex. His mouth was curling a bit at one corner. Meganerd was actually trying to smile!

Great, she said to herself. They've got to him, too! She, too, was finding it hard to keep worrying about the images. They were harmless, weren't they? In a way, they were pretty funny.

"Well, folks, it's not a virus. At least not a virus known to man," said Alex. Then he looked at Denny. "I mean, to persons."

"So what do we do now?" Mike wanted to know.

"Keep it, of course. Study it," said Alex.

"Not on my mom's computer, you don't," protested Denny.

"You can always download the thing from the remote site if you want to play around with it," Mike reminded Alex.

"True," said Alex. He leaned back in the chair. "Well, we can't find it or disinfect it," he replied. "Only way to get rid of it would be to wipe the computer's hard drive."

"You mean, wipe the entire memory?" asked Denny, horrified. "My mom would skin me alive!"

"And if you keep it the way it is?" Alex asked, peering at her through his cloudy glasses.

Denny swallowed hard. "Same thing," she admitted.

"So?" he prodded.

"I guess we'd better get rid of it," she said.

"Yeah, but how?" Mike cut in. "What do we do? Nuke the computer?"

Alex winced. "Does your mom have the CDs for the operating system and all the other 'ware that's on the drive?" he asked, turning to Denny.

"Yeah, I think so." Denny pointed to a pile of CDs on one of the shelves.

Alex went over and flipped through them quickly. "Yep, looks like everything's here. It can all be reinstalled once the drive is clear." He selected a CD and inserted it into the drive. Then he pressed a couple of keys and sat back, waiting.

Moments later, the Bouncing Nerds disappeared from the air and the screen went blank blue.

"Wow!" said Denny.

"That's it?" Mike asked.

Alex nodded. "It's a wipe," he said. "I rebooted off a system CD and reformatted the hard drive. That'll wipe out everything that's on it. Good-bye, virus."

"You're sure?" asked Denny.

"Sure I'm sure. Of course, your mom will have to reinstall all the other software from her purchase CDs, if she's into that kind of thing. Or you can get the dealer to do it."

Mike whooped, and the three of them exchanged high fives.

"Now, don't go downloading any more wild-eyed 'ware," said Alex from the doorway. He winked at Denny and closed the door behind him.

"He's not such a bad guy after all," said Denny.

"The Bouncing Nerds musta got to him," said Mike.

The next morning, Denny's mother was running late. "I've got to look really together today," she complained as she dashed around the kitchen. "My minister wants me to brief the Prime Minister about the policy paper I just did."

"Want me to finish feeding Grub?" Denny offered.

"Would you? Thanks!"

"C'mon, Grubbo. Open wide," Denny said, prodding his lips with a spoonful of cereal.

He didn't seem much interested in his breakfast. In fact, he kept looking around the room.

"'Oasers?" he asked hopefully.

"No more toasters," Denny said firmly, taking the opportunity to pop the spoon into his open mouth. "Ever."

After school Denny switched on the computer. The screen was still blank blue. She put in a call to the computer service company to reinstall the computer's software.

"What do you mean the hard disk has been wiped?" the guy on the phone wanted to know. "What stupid jerk did that?"

"Who knows?" said Denny, crossing her fingers behind her back. "Anyway, we have all the CD-ROM s. But we'd sorta rather someone else did the reinstalling."

"Okay, okay," he grumbled. "I'll send somebody out."

Denny wandered into the living room and turned on the TV. It was tuned to *Newsworld,* and she was about to change channels when she realized the House of Commons Question Period was being broadcast live.

I wonder if they're talking about Mom's policy stuff? she thought, sitting down on the edge of the couch. She tried to follow the debate. All she could figure out was that the Leader of the Opposition was all worked up about something.

He kept yelling and pointing his finger at the Prime Minister.

She heard her mother's key in the lock and went out to meet her. "Hi. How did your big deal policy thing go?" she asked, collecting Grub and skinning him out of his jacket.

Her mother beamed. "Great. Just great," she said. "My minister was really pleased at the way I briefed the PM. He's using some of the stuff I did in the House this afternoon."

Figuring this was a good moment, Denny said, "Uh, Mom? The computer's gone weird. I called the company and they're sending a service guy over."

Her mother groaned. "Oh, for heaven's sake. The darn thing's brand new!"

Denny went back to the living room, where Grub was sitting in front of the TV set. She looked around for the remote to change the channel.

"Pretty boring stuff, Grubster?" she said. "How about a touch of Barney?"

He grinned up at her. "'Oasers," he announced.

"Huh?" Denny whirled and scanned every corner of the room. "You're goofy, Grub. There aren't any toasters here."

He nodded and pointed at the TV screen. "'Oasers," he insisted.

Then she saw them. A bunch of toasters flapped past the end

of the Prime Minister's nose. He blinked and waved his hand in front of his face.

"Excuse me, Mr. Speaker. As I was saying . . ." He started to go on, then stopped again as more toasters plinked into view around him.

Now the Leader of the Opposition was getting to his feet. "Mr. Speaker, I protest. If this government thinks it can distract the Opposition by cheap tricks—" He fell silent as more and more toasters began to appear.

"Holy cow!" gasped Denny.

Then the picture disappeared from the screen for a moment. "We are experiencing temporary difficulties with our transmission," the TV announced. "Please do not adjust your set."

Voices babbled in the background, but she couldn't hear anything clearly.

Denny grabbed the phone and dialed. "Mike?" she said. "Turn on *Newsworld*. Never mind why, just do it! And tell Alex!"

She slammed down the receiver just as the picture came back on. The camera scanned the House of Commons, showing flights of toasters looping and tacking through the air. The Members of Parliament had poured down onto the floor of the House. Some looked dazed. Others were batting at the toasters. The Prime Minister and the Leader of the Opposition were standing next to each other. Oddly enough, both were grinning.

"Crazy toasters! They're getting to them, too," said Denny. "But how did they get there? It couldn't be . . ."

Her mother came into the room. "How's the PM's speech

going?" she asked. Then she stopped dead and stared at the screen. "Wha-a-a . . . ?" she gasped.

Denny was thinking furiously. "Mom?" she said after a minute. "That stuff you worked on. You printed it out, didn't you?"

"Of course not," her mother replied. "I saved it on the hard drive as I worked. When it was finished, I put it on a floppy disk and took it to work with me."

A disk! Her mother must have copied the virus along with her report!

"Did . . . did you give the disk to anyone?" she asked, afraid she knew the answer already.

"Sure," said her mother, still absorbed in the toasters. "I put it into my computer at work and e-mailed everyone at the Ministry so it could be copied as needed. I even copied the disk and gave it to the PM. He was going to input it into his laptop, he said."

And guess who used his laptop in the House this afternoon? Denny finished to herself. Oh, lordy!

She scrunched down into the couch cushions, her eyes glued on the screen. Some of the MPs were laughing together and slapping each other on the back. Others were just watching the toasters with blissed-out expressions on their faces.

"Those toasters. Aren't they like the ones on your screen-saver?" her mother asked.

"Uh . . . kinda," said Denny. Her mind was racing. The guy who invented the software intended this to happen! she thought dazedly. He put the virus there on purpose. He knows what the images do to people.

And all over the world, people like her were probably downloading the program through the Net and spreading it around. And everywhere there was a computer . . .

Lots of places had computers, didn't they? Not just governments and businesses. Armies and navies. And all their warplanes and ships and tanks.

Denny swallowed hard.

Her mother was smiling now as she watched the antics of the toasters. "This is crazy, isn't it?" she said, turning to Denny. "What on earth is happening?"

"I think peace just broke out," said Denny in a small voice.

She just hoped nobody would blame it on *her!*

C I T Y • O F • T H E • D E A D

Sparrow was being hunted. She knew it because some of the people who usually spoke to her weren't speaking now. They just pretended they didn't see her. Others, the brave ones, at least told her she'd better clear out before they turned their backs. They didn't say who was after her. They didn't have to.

But where should she go? Nowhere downtown was safe. Angel had eyes everywhere. She could get up to the freeway and hitch a ride out of town, sure. But, scared as she was, she wasn't ready to do that. For one thing, it was pretty risky. Sparrow knew what could happen to girls who got into cars with strange guys. She knew girls it had happened to.

Besides it was her town, too, she told herself as she vaulted over the entrance turnstile to the subway. She disappeared down the stairs to the northbound trains, the shouts of the security guard fading away behind her.

Sparrow knew she had a good thing going, a nice bit of turf where she did okay with her squeegee gig. Right downtown in the business district. Lots of guys in big sleek Beamers and

Mercedes. She made pretty good money most days—at least when the cops didn't turn up to run her off. It was enough to keep her fed and in warm clothing. So she didn't want to have to move and start all over again.

She had her routine just about perfect now. A quick jump into the street the instant the light changed. "Hi, I'm Sparrow," she'd say with a big smile and start right in washing. "Wash your wind-shield?" she'd ask a moment later with an even bigger grin. By then she'd be almost done. Of course, some of the drivers yelled at her and made her stop. Some just shrugged and let her finish and then refused to pay her. But others, lots of others, would give her a quarter, a dollar, two dollars, sometimes even more. A guy had given her a fifty once; that blew her away. Imagine having that much money! She'd spent the fifty on a down-filled jacket. Nothing too flashy; nothing she'd get swarmed for. But warm and thick.

Sparrow wasn't her real name, of course. But it had been a long time since she'd thought of herself as anyone else. It was her advertisement, her image. She was proud of it because she'd thought it up all by herself one day in the park. She'd been watching the cheeky city sparrows hopping right up to people to steal crumbs from their lunches, and she'd liked their nerve. Hey, that's me! she'd thought.

And now she was Sparrow-on-the-run. She swung onto the very last car of the train, and wrapped her wiry wrist around a pole to brace herself. She never sat down on the subway, hated being squeezed between people. She needed her space.

Sparrow had no idea where she'd get off. No use going all the way out to the 'burbs. Too much distance to cover and not the kind of customers she was used to. No big tippers out there, was the word on the street.

No, she'd have to get off somewhere soon and lie low for a while, hoping Angel would lose track of her. Or cool down. He did that sometimes, she knew. He'd rage at someone who'd crossed him, then act as if he'd never cared at all. But other times . . .

Sparrow shivered and shifted her backpack. It was really dumb of her to have done what she did. But something about that kid he was hustling bothered her. Elaine hadn't been on the street long, and she was just too young to know what he was up to. She actually thought Angel loved her—as if Angel could love anyone! Elaine just couldn't see beyond Angel's looks and smooth words.

It was hard to believe that someone so nice-looking and soft-spoken was, well, the way Angel was. He looked like he belonged on a Christmas card in a long white robe with wings. He knew it, too. Like Sparrow, Angel had named himself.

So when she saw him closing in on Elaine, first sweet-talking her and then starting to lean on her to work the streets for him, Sparrow decided she had to act. She'd done the worst thing a kid on the street could do. She'd called a social service worker she knew and said where Elaine was and where she'd run away from and what was going to happen to her if somebody didn't do something fast. So the social welfare people came and took Elaine away.

Now the buzz on the street was that Angel had figured out who'd put in the phone call and was going to do something major about it. That's why she had to disappear for a while.

Luckily, she had a little money tucked away in her backpack, along with her spray bottle and squeegee. Enough to keep her in food for a while.

Her real problem was where to sleep. Shelters were out, not that she ever stayed in them much. Sparrow considered that she'd worked hard for her jacket and her other gear, and she wasn't about to get them stolen by any hostel rat. Anyway, Angel had eyes and ears in all the shelters, and he'd track her down in no time if she set foot in one. So if she couldn't find a way to sneak through the back door of a building, she'd have to find a sidewalk grating with a little heat coming out of it, though there was pretty fierce competition for them this winter, she knew. At worst she might have to settle for nothing more than a corner out of the wind for a few nights. Just the thought of that made her shiver.

The subway train was running above ground now, and Sparrow stared out the window at unfamiliar streets and the backyards of houses. She was getting farther and farther away from the part of the city she knew, and though this was what she intended, it still made her feel fidgety. Lots of people thought the city was the same all the way through, but Sparrow knew better. There were cities within cities within cities, each with its own look and feel and special ways of doing things. To survive on the street, you had to pick up the pattern and go with it. That way you were visible only when you wanted to be and invisible the rest of the time.

I'll get off at the next stop, she told herself. No use going too far. I don't want to stick out like . . . like a giraffe in a herd of cows. She grinned, enjoying the image.

She popped out of the subway entrance, having forged her way up through the dense crowds pouring down the stairs. It was after five o'clock, and the street was jammed with rush hour traffic. Just her thing.

She whipped out her spray and squeegee and jumped off the curb. "Hi, I'm Sparrow," she sang out, grinning.

The guy behind the wheel scowled and motioned her off. When she kept on washing, he rolled down his window and yelled, "Get lost, kid!"

Jeez, what a grouch!

She ran over to another car. "Hi," she began again, but just then the light changed, and a chorus of horns made her leap for the curb.

She crossed the street to catch the traffic going the other way. Now, here was a good chance. A nice shiny compact car with a woman behind the wheel. Women didn't pay you the most, but they almost always gave you *something*.

"Hi!" said Sparrow, turning on her smile. She even tapped politely on the side window. "Wash your windshield?" she asked, going to work. The spray bottle did a pretty good job, though not quite as good as dipping the squeegee in a bucket the way she did when she was working her own turf. But the idea of the spray was all her own, and Sparrow was pleased with herself for thinking of it. It kept her mobile and that was important right now.

"Oh, for heaven's sake," the woman said, annoyed. "Are you people moving uptown now?" But she rolled down the window and fished in her purse for a few coins.

"Gee, thanks, lady!" said Sparrow, pretending to be pleased. "You have a nice evening now!" She pocketed the coins and spun away toward the curb. It was part of the service to leave customers feeling cheerful. After all, you might see them again sometime.

She scanned the intersection looking for her next customer, but instead noticed a cop on the corner across from her. He'd spotted her, too. Uh-oh. Time to fade. It used to be that when cops saw squeegee kids they just looked the other way. But now there was this new law against squeegeeing. It made Sparrow burn just thinking about it. Who were squeegee kids hurting anyway? Their customers got clean windshields, and the kids got a little money to live on. What was wrong with that? Why did a bunch of uptight jerks have to pass a law to spoil it all? Well, it wasn't going to stop her anyway!

Sparrow blended into the crowd and allowed herself to be carried down into the subway again. Then she followed the underpass and came back up on the opposite corner. Sure enough. The cop was standing right where she'd been, looking around for her. She popped her spray bottle and squeegee into her backpack and set off in the opposite direction, no evidence in sight.

The smell of French fries tweaked her nose. She hadn't eaten since morning, and she was getting pretty hungry. Sparrow considered. She had the money. No question about that. But how long was she going to have to lie low? Her money wouldn't last forever. After a moment she shrugged and pushed open the door to the burger joint. She could always get a bit of money together with her squeegee. She'd just have to keep on the move and watch out for the cops.

The jerk behind the counter gave her a fishy look. "You planning to order or what?" he asked, keeping a close eye on her hands.

How do they always seem to know about street kids? Sparrow wondered. It wasn't as if she was dirty or in rags. She made a big show of getting her money out.

"Yeah, I am. Okay?" she snapped, waving a five-dollar bill.

"Sure. Whatcha want?" he asked, polishing the counter with a none-too-clean cloth.

Sparrow took her time deciding. This was a big deal. She didn't often allow herself to eat in cafés, not even crummy ones like this. "Home burger with everything," she said at last. "Curly fries. With lots of vinegar."

When he turned to pass the order to the kitchen, she deftly pocketed a handful of ketchup packets. It was amazing how many things ketchup could improve.

She paid for her order and sat down in a booth away from the front windows. Not that she thought any of Angel's narcs would come looking for her this far uptown, but it didn't hurt to be careful.

When her order came, she picked up the burger and inhaled the smell, then closed her eyes and took a big bite, chewing luxuriously. This was living!

Someday when I get a little money together, I'll start a real business of my own, she promised herself. Then I'll eat out or send out for food every single day.

The hamburger disappeared too quickly. Sparrow briefly thought about ordering another; then her eyes lingered on the rack of doughnuts behind the counter. But she sighed and got up. She couldn't risk being greedy. Not when she'd been pushed off her turf.

She slung her backpack over her shoulder and sauntered toward the door, adding some relish and mustard packets to her pockets on the way. If the jerk wasn't smart enough to watch her on the way out like he had on the way in, it was his problem, right?

It was starting to get dark. Sparrow headed downhill, not sure what she should do next. Maybe she should start checking for vacant doorways in some of the office towers. Most people would have gone home by now. It wouldn't hurt to stake out a location and see if anyone dangerous-looking had it in mind, too.

She prowled around several buildings. A couple of them had security guards in the lobby. Bad luck. Those guys just wouldn't leave you alone. And the back doors of all the buildings she tried were locked. That was just another part of the problem of being off her turf, where she knew which guards were sloppy, which doors didn't close quite tight.

After a while she gave up on spending the night indoors. She went on searching until she found a heating grate in the angle of a wall along an alley. Not great, but it would do. She headed over and stood on the grate, toasting her toes.

Then a menacing voice said, "Don't even think about it, kid."

Sparrow whirled around. A bad-looking dude had padded up

the alley behind her. He had one hand in his pocket, and she did-n't want to find out what he had in it.

"Excu-u-u-use me!" she said, giving him a salute. She turned and jogged down the alley in the opposite direction.

When she was well away, she stopped and looked back. He hadn't followed her. Well, now what? The wind had an edge to it and she shivered. She didn't want to head back downtown too much more.

There was an open space a block ahead of her. A park? she wondered. Better to keep away from it. Lots of nasty things went on in parks at night. But it didn't look like a park, exactly. There were winding roads and buildings.

And gravestones. It was a cemetery, she realized. A great big fancy one. She'd never seen a graveyard with tombs that looked like funny little houses before.

Houses! she thought. Just what she was looking for, right? Sparrow chuckled. Lots of people might be put off by sleeping in a graveyard, but not her. Dead people were no problem. It was live people who caused you grief, wasn't it?

She trotted down the block and paused to look around. There was nobody to see her. Then she scaled the iron palings that sur-rounded the cemetery and dropped lightly to the ground on the other side.

There'd be a watchman or caretaker somewhere around, she knew. But she figured he'd likely be holed up in an office near the main gate on a cold night like this.

She got away from the streetlights at the edge of the cemetery as quickly as she could. No use being too visible. Her eyes soon adjusted to the dusk, and she had no trouble seeing her way.

The ground rose and fell in slopes and valleys. The tombs mostly sat on the tops of the slopes. Just like real houses, Sparrow thought. The guys with the money get the best view. Not that anyone here really needed a view, of course.

She went up a winding path to one of the houses. It was a classy-looking place with a domed roof and pillars at the front. Kind of like one of the old bank buildings downtown. The door was made of some sort of heavy metal. Sparrow pulled on the handle.

"Awww," she muttered, disappointed. It was locked. It hadn't occurred to her that anyone would lock up a tomb. Who'd want to steal dead bodies?

But Sparrow sighed in resignation. In this city, people would steal almost anything, in her experience.

There was another tomb on the slope across the way, so she jogged over and tried that. It was locked, too. Still she didn't give up hope. She moved on, deeper and deeper into the cemetery and farther from the glow of light along the street.

Five tombs later, she knew she was beaten. They were all locked. And there was no way she could spend the night outside here. The wind was cutting. She'd have to go back up the street and take her chances in some nonprime spot in an alley. She didn't like the thought of that. Sparrow didn't like sleeping that rough.

From where she was standing, she could just make out the shape of another tomb right in the center of the cemetery. She shrugged. Might as well try one more. What did she have to lose except a few more miserable moments on cold pavement?

She trotted over. This one had pillars, too, but the roof was flat. There was a statue to the right of the door. A huge crouching lion with its paws stretched out in front of it.

Sparrow checked the entrance, and her heart sank. It was blocked by a barred gate held in place by a heavy chain and padlock. "Rats!" she muttered.

In frustration, she gave the padlock a yank. With a click, it sprang open in her hand. Like magic.

"Yes!" she breathed, hardly able to believe her luck. Now, if only the inner doors weren't locked.

She unhooked the padlock and pulled the chain away from the gate, then pushed on the bars. The gate swung inward with a faint groan. The inner doors were held in place by a bolt. It slid back easily and she stepped inside.

It wasn't as dark as she'd thought it would be. Two small barred windows, high up on each side, let in some light. She sniffed cautiously. It didn't stink or anything. Just smelled sort of damp and musty.

In an inner chamber at the back she could see something big and bulky, like a king-size stone bathtub with a heavy lid. That must be where the body was. Other than that, the tomb was empty.

Would the owner mind her moving in? Sparrow didn't exactly believe in ghosts, but she didn't exactly not believe in them either. Anyway, it never hurt to be polite.

She put down her backpack and walked into the inner chamber. "Uh, excuse me?" she said to the stone bathtub. "Whoever you are? My name's Sparrow. I'm not going to make trouble or diss you or anything. I just need a place to stay tonight. Okay?"

She wasn't expecting an answer and there was none. But asking permission made her feel more comfortable somehow. As she turned to go, she glanced down at the stone lid. Even in the dim light she cold make out two dates carved into it in large figures: 1875-1925. Wow, thought Sparrow. Way olden times.

Back in the outer chamber, she pushed the barred gate closed and set the chain and padlock aside on the floor. The inner doors she left ajar. Despite having introduced herself, she wasn't keen on getting too cozy with the tomb's occupant.

She rummaged in her backpack and pulled out a thin mat and a thick wad of folded plastic garbage bags. Too bad there weren't any newspapers or cardboard boxes around, but the bags were a lot better than nothing. She laid out the mat and spread two bags over it. Then she slid her legs inside another bag and tore holes for her head and arms in a fourth. She pulled that on like a vest, lay down on the mat with her head pillowed on her backpack and arranged more bags over her as a coverlet.

It was pretty cold, but she'd warm up a bit under the bags. She curled up in a ball and wrapped her arms around herself. And at least she was out of the wind, she thought as she drifted off to sleep.

Sparrow dreamed.

She was under a sky of burning blue. High overhead, a bird with sharply pointed wings wheeled against the blazing disk of the sun. All around her stretched a dry rocky valley edged by low cliffs. The air shimmered with heat, and the ground was hot, too.

She could feel it right through the soles of her boots.

She looked down. The boots were adult, and her body was tall and broad. She was in a man's body!

The man strode toward a pile of rocks at the foot of one of the cliffs. As he got closer, Sparrow could see a square black hole leading into the ground. She could sense the man's thoughts, as though she were tucked away somewhere in a corner of his brain. No one had believed him when he said the tomb of Anenhotek must be here. Now he had found it, opened it. His name would be known around the world, and his fortune would be made by what lay inside the tomb. All he had to do now was locate the burial chamber.

A harsh scream split the desert air, and the man glanced up. A golden hawk was plummeting down at him, claws out-stretched. It slashed at him, then swooped back for another attack. He threw his arms up over his head and dashed down the stone steps that led into the tomb. When he looked back, the bird had veered along the cliffs, trying to regain height. It screamed again and disappeared over the rim of the valley.

Sparrow woke up sweating, the bird's cry echoing in her head. For a moment she stared into the dark, wondering where she was. Then she sat up and pulled off the garbage-bag vest. She lay down again and rearranged the rest of the bags.

It was funny how powerful the dream had been. She could still see the valley clearly when she closed her eyes. She could feel its burning heat, even though the air around her was bitterly cold. She remembered the thoughts of the man, too. He seemed so real. But what the heck was he doing in her dream? Who was he?

Just as she curled up again, a name came into her head, almost as if a voice had spoken it.

Cartwright.

She puzzled over it for a moment, then turned her face into her backpack and slept. This time there were no dreams.

She was up early the next morning. She didn't really expect anyone to come around checking the cemetery at that hour, but why take a chance? She refolded her gear and stuffed it into her backpack, making sure the spray bottle and squeegee were right on the top. Then she slung the pack over her shoulders and stepped out through the inner doors, pulling them snugly closed behind her and sliding the bolt across. Once outside, she closed the gate and looped the chain back through the bars.

She picked up the padlock and was about to snap it in place when a thought struck her. She'd probably be miles away from here by tonight, but . . . you never know, she told herself. So she hooked the lock through the links, being careful not to snap it shut, and tucked it out of sight behind the mass of the chain. Perfect. Nobody would notice that the lock was open.

Now that it was daylight, she could see that the lion guarding the entrance to the tomb wasn't all lion. It had a human face, and it wore some kind of headdress. She struggled to remember the right word for that kind of beast. She'd seen it in a picture book, way back in elementary school when she'd been doing a report about ancient Egypt. It was a . . . a . . .

Sphinx.

The unheard voice whispered the word in her mind. Sparrow stared at the stone beast as if it had spoken. It didn't look like some ancient god or king, Sparrow thought. It looked like an ordinary man with high cheekbones and a hooked nose. It lay there, eyes wide open, gazing down over the cemetery. There was something about its expression. Sorrow? No, more than that. Much more. The sphinx looked terrified, Sparrow thought, as if it had seen some dreadful thing. She could hardly tear her eyes away from its stricken gaze. When she did she saw the name "Cartwright" carved across its stony chest.

Cartwright! But that was the name she had heard in the night. She turned and stared back at the tomb. The same name was carved into the stone lintel over the door. It must be the name of the person buried in the stone bathtub. Maybe it was the name of the man in her dream, too! That would explain why she dreamed she was in a man's body.

A sudden thought chilled her. This guy Cartwright was haunting her! He'd got into her dream and showed her all that stuff about the hawk and the tomb he'd found. But why? Sparrow wondered. Just because she'd slept in his tomb? She looked down at the sphinx. The face must belong to Cartwright—who else would it be? But why did he look so terrified?

"If only you could talk, boy," she murmured, giving the sphinx a pat, "you could explain it all to me."

At that moment something swooped close overhead, so close that she ducked automatically. She caught a glimpse of a bird vanishing swiftly in the direction of the street. It reminded her of the hawk in the dream. But what would a hawk be doing in the city?

Sparrow shrugged. She had better get going. "G'bye,

Cartwright," she said to the sphinx. "Thanks for everything. Maybe I'll catch you later."

A light snow had fallen in the night. Sparrow broke a branch off one of the shrubs planted around the tomb, then moved backward down the path, carefully sweeping away her tracks as she went.

The light of the sun was just touching the tops of the tall buildings up the street. High up, a bird was circling. Its wings were pointed like those of the bird in the dream. She stopped and watched it for a minute. It landed on a ledge near the top of a building nearby and peered down at the cemetery. Almost as if it were keeping watch over something. Or somebody.

She hit the public washroom at the subway interchange. She figured it would be pretty safe this early on. She used the toilet, then washed her hands and splashed water on her face. She ran her wet hands through her short brown curls, and then she was done.

She surfaced and slipped up the alley behind the diner where she'd eaten the night before. She was in luck—the garbage had been put out. After glancing both ways, she undid a bag and peered inside. Not too bad, actually. Amazing what a lot of restaurants threw out every day, with people going hungry all around.

Sparrow whipped out one of her own bags and selected some delicacies. There was an untouched bun with a stiff hamburger patty inside it. Better keep that for dinner—just in case, she told herself, carefully stowing it away. Then her eyes lit up as she came across four slightly squashed chocolate doughnuts. They had a bit of ketchup on them, but who cared? She liked ketchup.

She took out the doughnuts and closed the bag up again. No use pushing her luck. She'd be willing to bet that someone else would be arriving to check out the garbage any minute. Good stuff like this didn't get left lying around for long.

She ate two of the doughnuts on a bench on the subway platform. Then she caught a westbound train. Better not keep hanging around the same place as yesterday, she thought. Not with that cop on the lookout for her.

All in all, she had a pretty good day. Not a sign of trouble; not a single cop to chase her off. She worked one intersection two stops over for a while, then headed farther west again. Later she caught an eastbound train past the main interchange and worked her way back.

She hadn't decided where to spend the night yet, but the thought of the tomb in the cemetery was lurking at the back of her mind. It was kind of nice to know there was a safe place waiting for her, even if it was haunted. Not that she was getting soft or anything!

She thought briefly of buying another meal, but decided to play it safe with her money. She'd done all right today, though. No big tips like the ones she sometimes got downtown, but she'd made about twenty dollars. Still, who could tell how long she'd have to stay away from her turf downtown?

Sparrow jumped off the train at the interchange and headed over to check the recycling boxes for newspapers. She stowed several crumpled ones in her backpack. The fresh-looking ones she smoothed and refolded. Then she moved among the people on the platform, offering the papers for a dime each. People never minded a bargain paper as long as it looked fresh.

When the rush hour was over, she bought herself a tin of cola and emerged into the street. Suddenly, her survival instincts shifted into high gear. There were some guys hanging around the subway entrance. Casual-looking guys—way too casual. What they were really doing was scanning the crowds for someone. Sparrow was sure of it. Her gaze moved over them coolly, not lingering for a single second, but she didn't miss a detail. She didn't recognize any of them, but that meant nothing. Angel probably had plenty of narcs she didn't know about.

She'd better get out of sight, just in case. She headed off in the direction opposite to the one she needed to go, then doubled back, cutting through alleys until she came out on the edge of the cemetery again.

She stood by the iron fence for a moment, remembering Cartwright in his tomb and the strange dream she'd had about him. Was he really haunting her? The thought was scary, but it also made her feel sort of . . . well, special, as if she mattered to someone, even if it was only an old ghost. Sparrow shrugged. At least the dream had kept her warm last night. And Cartwright wasn't trying to harm her, was he? Anyway, she had a lot worse things to worry about than spooks. There was no way she was going to let anything scare her away from a safe place to sleep. Especially when those guys at the subway might have caught sight of her.

Sparrow didn't try to enter the cemetery at the same place as before, but walked east until she found an entrance. The gate was still open, and she slipped in. Keeping off the main roads, she stayed on the narrower paths that wound their way across the grounds. She found Cartwright's tomb again with no trouble, even though it was getting dark. It almost seemed to be waiting for her. Strange.

"Hi, Cartwright," she said softly, giving the sphinx a pat. "It's only me. Hope you don't mind a return visit."

The lock and chain were just as she'd left them. Once inside, she laid out the newspapers and brought out her mat and garbage bags. Then she fished in the bottom of the backpack and pulled out her food bag, along with some of the ketchup and mustard she'd filched the day before.

The hamburger was cold and greasy, but Sparrow wolfed it down with plenty of ketchup and followed it up with the remaining doughnuts. She washed the meal down with the cola.

After building herself a proper nest out of the newspapers and garbage bags, she settled down and lay staring at the ceiling, waiting for something to happen. Though she was a bit nervous, she couldn't help being curious, too. She closed her eyes, trying to feel the burning heat of the desert valley again, to see the hawk circling high against the blue sky. After a while she slept.

She was in a dark enclosed passage, looking out of Cartwright's eyes again. He was holding a flashlight in his hand, swinging its beam back and forth ahead of him as he moved forward, as if he was searching for something. Wall paintings of golden-skinned dark-eyed people stared out as the light struck them, then vanished into the blackness as he passed.

The flashlight beam picked out a narrow passage leading off

to one side. Cartwright squeezed himself along it, shining the light ahead of him. Suddenly, the passage opened out into a shadowy chamber, and he caught his breath. A huge golden hawk loomed out of the dark, its eyes glaring, its wings outspread.

Sparrow was terrified, but Cartwright said softly, "Greetings, Horus." He shone the flashlight beam here and there, and slowly Sparrow understood what she was looking at. It was a burial chamber full of treasure more incredible than anything she had ever imagined. The great hawk that glared at Cartwright was made of gleaming gold, its wings spread protectively around a golden shrine. It almost seemed to Sparrow that she could see rage and despair in its enameled eyes, though it must only have been the flicker of the light across it.

Cartwright carefully examined a great seal across the doors of the shrine. He patted it, satisfied. "Unbroken," he murmured. "The mummy inside will be perfect. . . ." As he moved the flashlight, it picked out a row of strange images painted on the side of the shrine—a little bird that looked like the hawk, a man wearing a tall peaked crown, reeds, a boat, the disk of the sun. . . . They must have been a language because Cartwright leaned close, reading aloud as the light flashed across them:

"Read, and beware the doom of Horus. Cursed be he who disturbs the sleep of King Anenhotek. Awake shall he remain beyond the gates of death till pity melts his heart of stone."

Cartwright gave a low whistle. "A powerful curse, Horus," he said, turning to stare at the golden hawk. "But I don't believe in such superstitions."

He began to make his way back down the passage. Sparrow

thought she could almost feel the angry gaze of the hawk boring into his back as he left.

She awoke, gasping for air. It was so hot and stuffy underground. But the breath she drew in was icy cold. Then she remembered where she was.

Sparrow lay awake, puzzling it through. Cartwright must have been a scientist who studied tombs. He'd discovered the treasure of an ancient king and was going to take it away. And the hawk was angry, and there was a curse on the old king's tomb.

But why was Cartwright showing her all this stuff? It was over and done with long ago, wasn't it? Yet the dream had left her with an uneasy feeling, as if maybe it wasn't really over at all.

Then, like an answer to her question, a voice in her head echoed the words of the curse:

Awake shall he remain beyond the gates of death. . . .

Awake! Sparrow gulped, and her eyes flicked toward the stone container in the shadowy inner chamber. She yanked the garbage bags right up under her chin. Was Cartwright telling her he was still awake in there? But he couldn't be. His body must have crumbled into dust years ago!

"I . . . I know you're trying to tell me something," she whispered to the darkness. "But I don't understand."

Sphinxxx . . . The word was like a sigh, and then she saw a man's face with high cheekbones and a hooked nose take shape in the air before her.

"C-C-Cartwright?" breathed Sparrow.

But even as she watched, the man's eyes widened as if he had seen some dreadful thing. Slowly, his face froze into the stony countenance of the sphinx. Only the eyes remained alive, full of unspeakable horror. A moment later the vision faded, leaving only darkness.

Sparrow sat bolt upright. *The sphinx was awake!* That's what Cartwright was trying to tell her. The curse of Horus must have locked up Cartwright's spirit in the sphinx for all eternity. Unless—but how could pity melt a heart of stone? she wondered. And who would he pity?

She lay down again and squeezed her eyes shut, but there was no way she could sleep. Not now. She kept seeing the tomb, the angry hawk and the terror-stricken eyes of the sphinx. After a while she got up. Outside, the sky was clear and the moon hung low above the trees, bathing the sphinx in milky light. Shrinkingly, she approached it and gazed into its grim face. Was there really a flicker of life in the eyes or was it only the moon-light? Sparrow's fear turned to pity as she imagined it crouching there, awake for year after endless year, through sunshine and snowfall, never to rest, never to sleep. And nobody knew. Nobody would ever know—except her. Who else would be weird enough to believe it except a squeegee kid on the run?

Sparrow stroked the head of the sphinx. "Aw, Cartwright," she said softly. "I guess you just wanted someone to know about it all, and I'm the one. I wish I knew how to help you. But you should have left that old king alone!"

Yes-s-s-s . . .

A cold wind sighed through the bronze doors of the tomb, lifting the hair on the back of her neck. Sparrow shivered. At last she left the sphinx to its lonely vigil and curled up in her newspapers and garbage bags again. The next thing she knew, it was morning.

She started packing her bag, but stopped. Why bother to move out anyway? Now that she understood about Cartwright, the thought of him was more sad than scary. Maybe the poor old sphinx could use some company. So why not just count on coming back until something better turned up? She'd be safer here than sleeping rough on the street.

She folded the newspapers and garbage bags and piled them neatly out of sight behind the doors. It wouldn't do to have anyone notice she had moved in.

She went outside and stretched. "Good morning, Cartwright," she said, patting the sphinx. Suddenly, she felt as if she were being watched. She glanced down at the stone beast. "Is that you watching me?" she asked it. But its eyes were fixed on the graveyard below. She scanned the nearby slopes and valleys, but saw no one, and the snow near the tomb was unmarked by tracks other than hers.

Just nerves, she thought. What I need is breakfast. I'd better do something about my tracks, though. She repeated the same precautions as the day before, sweeping the path behind her as she went down toward the street.

That day she stayed away from the main subway interchange, just in case. She walked several blocks and took the subway out to the east end of the city. But she didn't do so well out there. People hadn't caught on to the windshield-washing idea. They just swore at her and refused to pay. One creep with a cell phone even put in a call to the cops, and she had to scuttle off.

Her garbage scrounging didn't work out either. All she found was stuff so gross that even ketchup couldn't save it. She had to dip into her hoard of money to buy food, but she didn't want to risk spending too much. So she bought a couple of day-old buns at a bakery for her dinner and promised herself that tomorrow she'd do better.

It seemed to be getting colder. Or maybe it was just that she hadn't had enough to eat. At any rate she was shivering as she made her way back to the cemetery at dusk. At Cartwright's tomb she greeted the sphinx and again found the lock as she had left it. The bolt on the inner doors was open, though, which puzzled her. She was pretty sure she had closed it.

I must be getting sloppy, she reproached herself. She pushed the doors open and stepped inside.

Out of the darkness, a familiar voice said, "Welcome home, Sparrow."

Angel!

Sparrow leaped back through the gates and sprinted down the hill. She could hear Angel close behind her, and she dodged just as he tackled her. She fell to the ground with Angel clawing at her backpack. She shrugged out of it, and was up and running in an instant. It was no use, she knew. He'd catch her long before she reached the street. And now other figures came running toward her. He had goons waiting.

Gasping for breath she shot off to the right and doubled back up the slope, not really thinking where she was going. She was just running for her life. When she reached the tomb, she sprang through the gate and slammed it behind her, gripping it fast with both hands. Panting, she turned and faced Angel.

He was breathing hard, too, and his face was an icy mask. "Now, that's a really stupid move," he said. "You know I can force the gate. I'm stronger than you. So why don't you just give up?"

Sparrow knew he was right. He'd get her for sure, unless . . .

The chain and lock still dangled through the bars. Could she pull the chain through and snap the lock? She'd have to be quick.

"Why don't you just leave me alone?" she yelled to distract him and moved her right hand slowly toward the chain.

He cocked his head, smiling down at her. "C'mon, Sparrow. You know why. Because you stuck your nose into my business. And I don't let anybody, especially smart-ass little girls like you, get away with that." He reached inside his jacket and pulled something out. A knife. The blade flicked out, gleaming in the waning light.

Sparrow grabbed the free end of the chain and looped it around the bars. Cursing, Angel leaped forward and started pulling on the chain from the other side. She could feel it slipping through her hands link by link. She sobbed and wrestled with the padlock, trying to hook it through the links and snap it shut.

Angel slashed at her through the bars with one hand, keeping up a steady pull on the chain. Sparrow yelped as the knife sliced into her hand. But the lock clicked shut. She shrank back from the bars and cradled her hand while Angel yanked on the lock, swearing. Sparrow held her breath. The lock had sprung open before when she pulled hard on it. If it gave way now . . . She whimpered and backed farther into the tomb.

But the lock held. Angel kicked the bars until they rattled. Then he swore at her viciously.

Sparrow sank down on the cold stone floor. I'm safe, she told herself dizzily, watching blood well up between her fingers.

In a moment Angel was cool again. It was terrifying the way his mood could change in seconds. "Well," he said, staring in at her through the bars. He flicked the knife shut and put it back inside his jacket. "So you've caged yourself." He began to smile as he thought it through. "Actually, it's pretty neat," he went on. "I won't have to do a thing."

Sparrow gazed back at him, openmouthed. She was beginning to shiver from shock.

"Are you cold, Sparrow? Hungry, maybe?" Angel went on. "You'd better get used to it, 'cause you're going to be plenty of both from now on."

Through her numbness, Sparrow dimly understood what he was saying. He was going to leave her in there to freeze or starve!

"You can't—" she began.

Angel grinned. "But I didn't. You did it to yourself. That's the beauty of it! And don't think that anyone will come by to rescue you. I've been watching this place since one of my guys saw you heading this way. Nobody comes here. The old fool of a caretaker just sits in his hut and keeps his toes warm."

Sparrow stared at him silently through the bars. It was no use begging for mercy. No use at all.

Angel turned away. "Well, bye for now, kid," he said over his shoulder. "Maybe I'll drop by later. I'll even bring some food." He chuckled. "You can watch me eat it."

Then he stopped and turned around. "Oh, and Sparrow, you remember Elaine?" he asked. "The little punk you tried to rescue? Well, the jerks at social services didn't keep a close eye on her, and she ran right back to me. She's turning tricks for me now, just the way I planned. So you got yourself all this grief for nothing."

He turned and went down the path, and other figures appeared out of the dusk to join him. Angel picked up Sparrow's backpack and held it up mockingly before he and the others disappeared toward the street.

They had the place staked out, Sparrow thought dully, watching them go. I never had a chance.

Her hand throbbed painfully. The cut was deep and ugly, and it gaped open in a way that made her feel sick just looking at it. Blood still oozed from the wound, and Sparrow knew she'd have to try to do something. If only I still had my backpack, she thought.

After a struggle, she managed to tear a strip off the bottom of her shirt and wrap it around her hand. Using her teeth and her good hand, she managed a kind of knot to hold the piece of cloth in place. But the cut went on bleeding, and a red stain began to soak though the bandage.

What am I going to do? she thought. What *can* I do? She was terribly cold, and the pain of her wound made her feel faint. She pushed the inner doors shut to keep out the wind and got out the newspapers and garbage bags to make her nest. Then she curled up, trying to keep warm.

After a while she felt almost as if she were floating, and she wasn't so cold anymore. She dreamed of a clear blue sky with the hawk circling. It came lower and flew right over her, its fierce yellow eyes glaring into her face. She seemed to hear the voice she'd heard before.

. . . *till pity melts his heart of stone.*

"Don't be angry anymore, Horus," she pleaded, half waking. The yellow eyes vanished, and instead she seemed to see before her the terrible eyes of the sphinx. "Help me, Cartwright!" she whispered. "Please help me!" Then she drifted into darkness and felt nothing at all.

She woke at dawn. Someone was rattling the bars outside.

Angel had come back. And he must have a key! She could hear it grating in the lock.

"No," she whimpered, cowering against the wall. "Please, no."

The inner doors were flung back, and an old man with whiskers stared in at her. "What are you doing in here, you crazy kid?" he demanded. He seemed more puzzled than angry. Sparrow tried to get up, but she couldn't. He had to help her up and walk her outside.

"Are . . . are you the caretaker?" she asked.

He nodded. Then his eyes widened as he noticed her blood-soaked hand and clothing. He jerked a walkie-talkie out of his belt and spoke rapidly into it, "Hey, do you read me? We've got another one. Yeah, at the Cartwright mausoleum. No, this one's alive, but she's bleeding. Send the ambulance."

Sparrow leaned weakly against the sphinx. "How did you know?" she asked. "How did you find me?"

The caretaker didn't say anything for a moment. Then,

"Something brought me . . . sort of," he said in a funny voice.

Jeez, he looked almost as shaky as she felt. Almost as if he was terrified of something. But what? Sparrow wondered dizzily.

"I was in the hut out by the main gate," the old man went on. "Must have dropped off to sleep. I heard a scream. I jumped up and then there was a crash, like something real heavy hitting the front of the hut. When I opened the door there was nothing there. But there were big deep scratches—claw marks—down the door and paw prints in the snow, leading away."

"Paw prints?"

"Big ones. Like some giant cat's. Then I heard sirens and saw police cars at the gate. So I ran down there, and a guy had been killed." He shuddered. "It was pretty horrible," he went on. "It looked like he'd been clawed to death by some kind of beast."

"The guy," whispered Sparrow. "The one who . . . was he blond, good-looking?"

"He was blond all right," said the caretaker, frowning. "But he sure wasn't good-looking. Not anymore anyway."

Angel! thought Sparrow. He did come back! "But what made you come looking way up here?" she faltered.

The caretaker pointed. "I followed those," he said. "It was like I *had* to do it, I just had the strangest feeling."

They both stared at the double set of deep pug marks leading away from the statue and back again.

"You mean the sphinx made them?" cried Sparrow. "But . . . but it couldn't go anywhere! How could it?"

The caretaker shrugged. "I ain't sayin' nothin' about what I think," he said. "And if you're smart you won't neither."

She could hear the wail of a siren, getting closer now.

"C'mon, kid. Let's get you out of here." He put his arm around her shoulder and helped her down the path toward the road. At the bottom of the slope, Sparrow turned and looked back.

The sphinx lay basking in the first rays of the rising sun. But something about it had changed. Its eyes were closed now, and its expression was serene. And the tips of its stony claws were stained with blood.

SHARON STEWART was born in Kamloops, British Columbia. After studying history at university, she turned her sights toward the writing life—a childhood ambition that reemerged as she began editing for educational publishers. She has worked as an editor and writer for twenty years, and her stories and poems have appeared in many anthologies. She is the author of several young adult novels, including *The Minstrel Boy*, a timeslip Arthurian story; *The Dark Tower*, an historical novel about the daughter of Louis XVI; and *Spider's Web*, a contemporary story about a girl who discovers what it means to have real friends when she begins exploring the Internet. While spending a year in Pamplona, Spain, where her husband taught English, Sharon Stewart wrote her fourth novel, *My Anastasia*. Upon returning to Canada, she completed a contemporary novel, *Angel Fire*, and is at work on *Skydancer*, an animal fantasy novel.